'We're proud of our successes here. Harder-Kulm psychotherapy is reputedly amongst the best in the world. Dr Peterson is highly respected.' With a sly glance, Sister Madigan added, 'What do you think of him?'

The question took Joanne by surprise. 'I—I only met him last night. He seems very nice.' It sounded so fatuous. Intimidating would have been a more honest description.

The sister laughed as she tucked a stray strand of red hair behind her ear. 'It usually takes less time than that for a new nurse to fall head over heels in love with Dr Peterson,' she said dryly. 'Not to mention a few of our glamorous and not so glamorous clients. Daniel has oodles of sex appeal. Surely you must have noticed!'

'I was too tired last night to notice anything!' Joanne told her, but that wasn't strictly true. Daniel had had a rather disturbing effect on her, which she wasn't ready to admit even to herself. . .

Judith Worthy lives in an outer suburb of Melbourne, Australia, with her husband. When not writing she can usually be found bird-watching or gardening. She also likes to listen to music and the radio, paints a little, likes to travel and is concerned about conservation and animal cruelty. As well as romantic fiction, she also writes books for children. CONFIDENTIAL NURSE is Judith Worthy's twelfth Doctor Nurse Romance.

CONFIDENTIAL NURSE

BY

JUDITH WORTHY

MILLS & BOON LIMITED
ETON HOUSE 18-24 PARADISE ROAD
RICHMOND SURREY TW9 1SR

*First published in Great Britain 1987
by Mills & Boon Limited*

© Judith Worthy 1987

*Australian copyright 1987
Philippine copyright 1987*

ISBN 0 263 75949 0

*Set in Scantext Times Roman 10 on 11.5 pt.
03—1287—57481*

*Typeset in Great Britain by
Keene Graphics Ltd
Printed and bound in Great Britain by
Collins, Glasgow*

CHAPTER ONE

JOANNE began to suspect she'd made a mistake the minute the train pulled out of Interlaken West, leaving the town centre behind. Nearly everyone had left her carriage there; only a couple of Swiss businessmen had remained besides herself to travel on to the last stop, Interlaken Ost.

By the time Joanne realised there was no one to meet her at Ost, and that she had confused 'east' and 'west', the railway station was deserted. Even the ticket window was very firmly closed.

For a few moments she stood in the empty station yard wondering what to do. It had been a long and frustrating journey from London, starting with a strike at Heathrow which had delayed her plans and made her miss her rail connections, and she was feeling very tired and rather jaded.

However, since there was nothing else she could do, she set off along the dark, empty road in, she hoped, the right direction. Snow was falling lightly and she was soon chilled to the bone, despite the warm clothing she was wearing.

'I must be stark raving mad!' she muttered. Her suitcase bumped against her leg, making walking slow and difficult.

All the more so, she thought ruefully, since she wasn't even sure that the nursing job she was going to was right for her. Perhaps, in her rather churned-up state, she had been hasty about accepting it.

'Just as long as this is the way back to town,' she said to herself as she stopped and switched the suitcase to the other hand.

She had only walked a few more steps when the scarf she had wound around her neck and across her nose and mouth to keep out the cold slipped. She stopped again to tie it on more firmly and as she did so a sleek grey car came up behind her and braked.

'*Kann ich Ihnen helfen, Fräulein?*'

The guttural male voice crackled across the crisp night air.

Rather nervously, Joanne replied, '*Nein, danke.*' Her teeth were chattering so much she could hardly speak.

The driver of the Mercedes got out. He was a large broad-shouldered man in a sheepskin-lined jacket with the collar turned up. He loomed forbiddingly over her and Joanne was acutely aware of being appraised by deep-set eyes shadowed by heavily brooding brows, even though she could not see them clearly. He had thick dark hair and a rather stern mouth that seemed to Joanne to quiver with impatience. She was obviously holding him up.

'English?' he queried brusquely in that language.

'Yes.'

'Isn't it rather late for going for a walk in the snow?' He noticed her suitcase and added with a touch of sarcasm, 'Have you been thrown out of your *pension?*'

But who would do that on such a night? he was thinking. And surely she couldn't have done anything to deserve it, not this rather appealing little figure with her pale oval face, the snow sparkling on long curling lashes and the waves of brown hair that flowed from under a rather rakish knitted hat. Her lips were quivering with fatigue and cold, but her eyes showed a determined spirit and there was a very independent tilt to her chin. She was also wary of him.

Joanne's astonishment at his perfect English, with no trace of accent, almost overrode her indignation, but she burst out, 'No! I—I made a mistake over the stations. I don't know why, but I thought Ost must be the town centre, and when we stopped at West I just didn't realise my mistake in time, and I. . .' Suddenly tears of frustration burned her eyes and she began shivering violently with suppressed emotion and the cold which was even more biting now she wasn't walking. 'I must find a phone and let them know. . .' she stammered. 'Someone was to have met me and. . .'

Her voice gave out as a large hand dropped heavily on her shoulder. 'Good grief!' he exclaimed. 'Is it possible. . .?' He drew in a sharp breath. 'Are *you* the nurse my mother engaged in London?' He sounded as incredulous as she did herself when she exclaimed,

' *Your* mother!'

He must have felt the tremors running through her, because he said more kindly, 'Get in the car. You're nearly frozen, and no wonder.' As Joanne tried to lift her suitcase with numbed fingers, he took it from her. 'Here, give it to me!'

Joanne, bewildered but relieved to have been rescued so opportunely, slipped thankfully into the passenger seat. The warmth of the car's interior made her tingle all through, and by the time he had stowed her luggage in the boot and slid in beside her, feeling was already beginning to return to her fingers.

He turned to examine her better in the glow from the roof-light and she saw that he was more ruggedly good-looking than she had first supposed. What colour his eyes were she could not tell, shadowed as they were by thick lashes, but she felt the intensity of his look and averted her gaze.

'What's your name?' he asked. 'I've forgotten.'

That made her feel very small and insignificant. 'Joanne Courtney.'

'Yes, of course, I remember now.' He smiled suddenly, but a little loftily, she thought. Of course he must think her a complete idiot. 'You do seem to have made rather an unfortunate start,' he observed.

Joanne resented the fact that he seemed to be blaming her for everything, but she felt guilty nevertheless and said, 'I'm sorry. It was stupid of me to confuse the stations, and when we stopped at West I was only half awake... Oh, you must think I'm an idiot!'

He was regarding her intently and lifted one eyebrow mockingly. 'You said it, not me!'

Joanne did not care for his superior manner, nor the way his close proximity unnerved her a little. She could see now a faint resemblance to the tall, elegant woman who had interviewed her in London for the job at the Harder-Kulm Clinic. Dr Ahlberg-Peterson's son would not suffer fools gladly either, she thought with a sinking heart.

He said, 'Just as well I came along when I did. You'd have probably killed yourself lugging that heavy case all the way back to town. Why didn't you phone for a taxi?'

'The taxi-phone was locked and by the time I went back to the office to ask someone to help, that was closed too. Mine was the last train tonight, you see.'

Her honesty was disturbingly beguiling and he said rather gruffly, 'Isn't there a pay-phone?'

Joanne felt needled that he seemed to think her totally lacking in initiative. 'Yes, but I didn't have any change.' Tears pricked her eyes again. She was very tired and the unpheavals of the past few weeks were finally taking their toll. She was prepared for it to take time to adjust to her new life, but starting off so badly was making it more difficult already.

He gave her a steady look. 'Your journey seems to have been a chapter of mishaps from beginning to end. I trust you're not accident-prone.' She certainly didn't seem to be the competent, self-assured young woman his mother had described.

Joanne could think of nothing to say that would wipe the

supercilious look off his face which she would dearly have liked to do. She just said wearily, 'It was a stroke of good luck your coming along, Herr Ahlberg-Peterson.'

A flicker of a smile moved his rather stern mouth. 'Not really. When you phoned to say you were delayed, my mother asked me to meet you as she couldn't make it herself later, but unfortunately I was delayed in Lucerne. I was afraid you'd be becoming very impatient or thinking you'd been forgotten. I was on the way to Interlaken West when I spotted you.' He chuckled and said, 'It hasn't been our day, has it?'

His quiet laughter sent an unexpected tingle down her spine and she found herself laughing too as his sudden change of tone released some of her tension. No wonder he was a bit brusque, if he'd had a trying day too. 'It certainly seems like it,' she murmured.

He revved the engine and smoothly put the car into gear, saying, 'Well, I'd better get you home before you freeze to death!'

As the snow was still falling steadily, he switched on the windscreen wipers. Ahead of them the snow was settling in a white blanket on the road and Joanne was thankful not to be still trudging through it.

'I'm quite warm now,' she said.

Already the warmth of the car's interior and the rhythm of the wipers had begun to make her feel sleepy, and she hardly noticed as they drove through the town. Beyond, they seemed to enter a tunnel of darkness, relieved only by the headlights reflecting back from the snow and occasional lights of habitation. Joanne knew they were surrounded by mountains, but in the darkness there was nothing to be seen of them.

Her companion's voice suddenly jolted her back to awareness of him. 'By the way, my name is just Peterson— Daniel Peterson. My mother uses her maiden name as well as my father's.'

'You sound English,' Joanne ventured curiously.

'I'm half and half. My mother is Swiss and my father was English. I benefited greatly from being brought up in a bilingual household.'

As the thought occurred to her, Joanne asked, 'Are you a doctor too?'

'I'm a psychiatrist.'

'Are you—I mean do you. . .?' Tiredness was making her fumble with words.

'Am I part of the Harder-Kulm Clinic? Yes, it's a family affair. I also have a practice in Berne where I am three days a week. The clinic therefore has a resident psychiatrist as well as my mother. . .' He paused and glanced at her. 'No doubt there's quite a lot my mother didn't tell you, for fairly obvious reasons, but I think you're too exhausted now to be bothered with detail. It can wait till morning.'

Joanne did not argue. She was remembering, with some trepidation, the ice-blue eyes of Dr Ahlberg-Peterson, whose gaze had been so penetrating, whose questions had been so precise. At the interview, Joanne had been convinced she was not making a good impression, and afterwards had confessed as much to the woman at the employment agency. The consultant had said, 'I agree she doesn't seem the kind to suffer fools gladly, but you never know! She needs to be very fussy, of course, very sure she can trust whoever she employs, but of course she must have explained all that to you.'

Dr Ahlberg-Peterson had. The Harder-Kulm Clinic's patients were often very well-known people who wished to avoid having their illnesses made public, and it was essential that anyone who worked there respected the privacy of the patients. It wasn't unusual for staff to be badgered by a curious press on occasions, Joanne had been told.

Joanne hadn't been sure she wanted to switch from the NHS to nursing in a private clinic in Switzerland. She'd had many misgivings about it, but Terri, her father's new wife, had said reassuringly, 'It'll be great experience, Joanne, as well as a nice change for you.'

And a great escape, Joanne had thought to herself, an ideal solution to her problems. Nevertheless, she'd been very surprised to get the job and not sure whether she was as pleased as Terri expected her to be.

In the warmth of the car, her thoughts became muzzy until she was unable to prevent the drowsiness creeping over her and her head lolled against Daniel Peterson's shoulder and she slept.

'Joanne, wake up—we've arrived!'

The deep, gently insistent voice jerked her awake. She was mortified to find she had fallen asleep leaning against him. His face was very close to hers, but she still couldn't tell whether his eyes were light blue like his mother's or darker. His hand on her arm ceased its gently shaking, but his fingers still clasped her sleeve.

'We're here,' he said, in the indulgent tone he might normally use for a child.

Joanne sat bolt upright. 'I—I'm so sorry—I must have dropped off.'

First she'd been stupid, now she'd been weak. It hardly added up to a good impression, she thought, furious with herself for succumbing to the soporific effect of the warm car and the weariness induced by her long frustrating journey.

Through the car window she could partly discern the building in front of which they were parked. It looked like a large house with gables and a long balcony across the outside of the upper rooms which all seemed to be in darkness. A mellow glow from an overhead lamp illuminated the front porch and allowed her to see that the downstairs windows were shuttered. It wasn't quite what she had expected.

'Is this the clinic?' she asked.

'No, of course not. This is our house.'

'Your house? But I. . .' Joanne was startled.

He looked quizzically at her. 'You weren't told you would be living here?' Then he nodded with sudden understanding. 'No, she would have been circumspect, naturally.' He levelled an intensely penetrating look at her again. 'Actually, this is my mother's house, but I live here too when I'm not in Berne.' He looked thoughtful for a moment. 'As you didn't know you would be living *en famille*, then presumably your—er—dual function was not explained?'

'Dual function? What do you mean?' demanded Joanne, perplexed. 'I was engaged to be a nurse at the Harder-Kulm Clinic. Is there something else?' She was not a little dismayed by the mystery that now seemed to surround her appointment.

Daniel Peterson let out a long slow breath. 'I see. Well, I suppose she might have been afraid of putting you off.' He seemed to be talking to himself more than her.

'Please, what are you talking about?' Joanne asked nervously.

He patted her arm. 'Not now. You're tired and cold. You need a hot drink and a warm bed. Come on.'

Joanne, feeling thoroughly disconcerted now, got out of the car and crunched across the fresh snow to the porch while Daniel Peterson retrieved her suitcase from the boot. By the time he joined her, the door was open and Dr Ahlberg-Peterson was smiling a welcome.

To Joanne's surprise she slid her arm around her shoulders and pulled her inside. 'My dear, at last! I expected to find you here already when I got home. I've been so worried wondering what could have happened.'

She seemed not at all intimidating now, and Joanne relaxed a little. The blue eyes were friendly and welcoming and the stiff professional manner of the woman who had interviewed her in London was greatly softened.

Her son said, 'She's had a problem day, Mama. I suggest she has a hot drink and goes to bed at once. I'll take her luggage up.'

'Thank you, Daniel,' replied his mother, and with both hands clasping Joanne's, looked concernedly into her face. 'Poor child, you're almost asleep on your feet. Come along. I'll show you your room. We'll talk about everything tomorrow.'

Joanne was too weary to insist on explanations right then, despite her underlying anxiety which Daniel Peterson's remarks had aroused. Obediently she followed them upstairs, and as soon as they left her, undressed. When she emerged from the small bathroom adjoining her bedroom a few minutes later, Dr Ahlberg-Peterson was setting a hot drink beside the bed.

'I'm sure you won't need it to help you sleep,' she said with a smile, 'but have it anyway. It will warm you.'

Joanne had thawed out nicely in Daniel Peterson's car and was no longer chilled, but she thanked her new employer for the drink, and although she was tempted to ask questions, she did not, sensing that they would be firmly turned aside. Instead she resolved to contain her impatience until morning, and said good night.

As Dr Ahlberg-Peterson closed the bedroom door and Joanne pulled back the thick continental quilt covering the bed, voices carried briefly to her from outside.

Daniel and his mother were speaking German now, perhaps not realising how good a command of the language Joanne had since so far they had conversed only in English with her.

Daniel was saying, 'I'm not at all sure she's suitable. She

seems a bit *flatterhaft* to me, and in such a delicate situation she might do more harm than good.'

His mother replied, 'I wouldn't have thought so, Daniel. She has excellent references. But—well, we'll have to see. She's here now.'

'And we can send her packing if she proves unsuitable,' said Daniel dismissively, and in a tone that suggested he believed that would be proved very quickly.

The voices faded as they moved away. Joanne stared grimly at the bedroom door. There was one word she did not know—*flatterhaft*. She rummaged for her dictionary. 'Flighty—fickle—scatterbrained!' she whispered, burning with indignation. How dared he! Just because she'd made a stupid mistake over the names of the railway stations. Anyone could have done that.

She slipped into bed and sipped her milk drink. Suddenly there was a leaden feeling in her stomach. Taking on this job had been a mistake: every minute seemed to be proving it. She should have listened to her subconscious instead of to Terri.

Presently, still awake and staring at the ceiling in the dark, and her tiredness having mysteriously evaporated, Joanne was still thinking about Daniel Peterson's disparaging reference to her as 'a bit scatterbrained' and wondering what he had meant by 'a delicate situation'. Fortunately her wakefulness did not last long. The soft bed, the lightness and cosy warmth of the *doona*, soon beguiled her into a deep and dreamless sleep.

CHAPTER TWO

WHEN Joanne opened the shutters and looked out of her window next morning almost as soon as it was light, she gave a delighted gasp. The snow had stopped and the sky was misty pink. The view of mountains, lake and forests was breathtaking.

The nearest mountains seemed almost within touching distance. Their lower slopes were thickly clad with conifers and the tree branches were weighed down with scoops of snow. Above, the more distant snowy peaks were sharply etched against the sky. As Joanne stood drinking in this magnificence, the first shaft of sunlight reached the highest peak and illuminated it like a theatrical spotlight.

Joanne heaved a little sigh. She loved Switzerland, she had spent several holidays in the country and enjoyed skiing. But she had usually been to Davos. This was her first visit to the Bernese Oberland.

It had been partly her fondness for the country and skiing plus her fairly fluent German that had persuaded her to apply for the job at the Harder-Kulm Clinic when Terri had shown her the advertisement. There had also been her need to branch out in a new direction now that her father had married again, and her relationship with Luke seemed to have foundered.

Ever since her mother had died ten years before, Joanne had combined the onerous tasks of both full-time student and later staff nurse, and housekeeper for her father. Now Andrew Courtney had no need of her any longer. She was free to do as she wished.

It had been difficult at first, however, to convince her father and Terri that she really wanted to work abroad for a change and that she didn't feel she was being pushed out of her home.

'This is still your home,' Terri had insisted anxiously. 'You don't have to go because of me.' Terri was nearer Joanne's age than her husband's, which made her uncertain of Joanne's acceptance, despite Joanne's assurance that she was delighted with the marriage.

Joanne simply felt that she had reached a crossroads in her life. She had been working for a long time at the Lord Barmouth Psychiatric Hospital just outside London and she felt she needed a change. She needed it as much because of Luke as anything else.

She needed, in fact, to adjust herself to the fact that nothing was going to come of her relationship with Luke Frensham, the man she had once thought she would marry.

When he had obtained a post in a large institution in America, he asked her to marry him and go too. She had believed herself in love with him and the temptation had been strong, but how could she leave her father? Luke said she had her own life to lead and if she loved him she would go. But Joanne had not been able to bring herself to do it.

She had asked Luke to wait to get married until he came back. They had argued about it, but Joanne had stood firm. If he loved her, he would wait. As there had been no formal engagement, there had been no formal breaking off, but after a few months Luke's letters had been briefer, with longer intervals between, and Joanne hadn't heard from him at all since she'd written to tell him that her father was remarrying.

That was what hurt. He obviously didn't want her as much as he had before. Perhaps she couldn't blame him. Perhaps two years was too long to ask a man to wait.

Lately she had toyed with the idea of following him to America just to find out how things really stood, but she couldn't bring herself to do that and risk a cruel rebuff. He might have someone else now. People at the Barmouth who knew about her and Luke sometimes asked about him, and not being able to answer truthfully gave her another reason for wanting to get away from it all.

She smiled wryly as she remembered Terri saying gaily when Joanne had confided her misgivings about the job, 'Think of it as a new beginning. Maybe you'll meet a handsome psychiatrist or a rich Swiss banker and get married too!'

Joanne had shrugged. She wasn't bitter about Luke, but she didn't feel in the least inclined to get involved with any man at the moment.

A tap at her door dragged her away from the window, and she called boldly in German, *'Herein!'*

An elderly woman entered with a breakfast tray which she placed on the table near the window. She regarded Joanne with sharp, inquisitive eyes. *'Guten Morgen,'* she said, without smiling.

'Guten Morgen,' Joanne replied, and when she went on in German, asking about the weather, a faint smile began to stretch the wrinkled old face.

Joanne was not familiar with Swiss-German dialects, but she was able to understand the woman's reply well enough.

Then she asked, 'Are you *das Haushälterin?'*

'Ja, ja! For many years.' Her smile stretched a little wider with pride and she smoothed her dark woollen dress with spread palms. 'I am Fräulein Müller,' she said in English, obviously proud of her knowledge of the language.

Joanne said, 'Thank you very much for bringing my breakfast, Fräulein Müller. I wasn't expecting that.'

'Bitte,' replied the housekeeper briefly. She retreated to

the door, saying, 'Tomorrow Elke will bring *das Frühstück*. She is not here today.' There was a slight pause before she added, as though just remembering, 'Gnädige Frau Luise asks you to come down to the study when you are ready. She said there is no hurry.'

'Tell her I won't be long,' said Joanne eagerly, resolved to start her day with at least one good impression.

After Fräulein Müller had gone, Joanne ate her breakfast quickly and resisted the temptation to linger over a second cup of coffee, while the sunlight crept over the face of the mountain visible through her window.

She showered and dressed in a green woollen dress and jacket which deepened the colour of her eyes and gave her light brown hair richer tones. She hoped it would be appropriate. Uniforms were not worn at the clinic, so she had not brought any. Uniforms were seldom worn at the Barmouth either.

A touch of orange-brown lipstick and a light whisk of mascara on her lashes were all the make-up Joanne needed, for she had the kind of complexion that needed little enhancing. Her hair was smoothly drawn back with side combs but tumbled over her forehead in a bouncy fringe.

Feeling a mixture of nervousness and anticipation, and with Daniel Peterson's uncomplimentary remarks still burning at the back of her brain, Joanne went downstairs. She was able this morning to take in more thoroughly her very pleasant surroundings. The house was spacious and elegantly furnished in a subdued but stylish way. Joanne's impression was of inhabitants who liked simple, practical things and as little clutter as possible. There was an all-pervading scent of pine-perfumed furniture polish that helped create a fresh clean atmosphere.

Joanne paused briefly on the stairs because two paintings caught her eye. Abstracts were not normally her favourites, but the brilliant colours and lively composition of these riveted her gaze. Someone with a wonderfully ebullient personality must have painted them, she thought idly.

As she turned away, to continue on down the stairs, she saw that she was being observed from below by a young woman in jeans with jet black hair sweeping slender shoulders and framing a pale but finely sculpted face. The girl's large grey-blue eyes startled Joanne with their intense but curiously expressionless gaze.

'*Guten Morgen,*' said Joanne as she came level with the girl.

The girl's gaze was fixed unwaveringly on her face. 'What are you doing here?' she asked imperiously, as though she suspected Joanne was an intruder.

'I'm Joanne Courtney,' Joanne replied. 'Doctor Peterson brought me here last night. . .'

Before she could explain further, the girl interrupted with a harsh little laugh.

'Daniel brought you? Oh, I see! You're another one of Daniel's women.' There was a touch of malice in her tone.

Joanne was shocked. 'I'm certainly not that!' she replied. 'I'm the new nurse for the clinic.' Boldly she added, 'Who are you?'

He entered so quietly that Joanne was not aware of anyone else in the spacious hallway until Daniel Peterson said, 'Good morning, Miss Courtney—' *Morgen*, Marie-Claire.'

Both girls turned to the man who had joined them. Last night he had called her Joanne, Joanne recalled. Why so formal this morning? Had he already persuaded his mother to send her back? His eyes were a deep grey-blue, she now discovered as they met hers in a look that said nothing, but although not as steely as she might have expected, was still decidedly uncompromising.

'This is my sister, Marie-Claire Valli,' said Daniel. 'Marie-Claire, Miss Courtney is our new. . .'

'Yes, she just told me,' interrupted Marie-Claire, following his lead and switching to English. She ignored both his greeting and Joanne's and pulled at the sleeves of her rather scruffy sweater while glowering at them both. Then, with a toss of her dark hair, and lifting her finely arched eyebrows, she gave a mocking little smile and remarked, 'Well, at least she's prettier than all the others!' Then she abruptly left them and went upstairs.

Daniel's lips compressed and Joanne felt the tension crackling in the atmosphere. She said nothing and neither did he. He took her arm lightly and enquired, 'Did you sleep well, and have you had breakfast?'

'I slept very well, thank you,' Joanne replied. 'And breakfast in my room was a luxury I wasn't expecting.'

'How well do you speak German?' he asked as he guided her across the hallway.

'Fairly well, but not fluently,' she answered modestly, 'and I'm a bit lost with dialects.'

'Don't worry,' he assured her, 'we'll speak English most of the time!'

He ushered her into his mother's study. Dr Ahlberg-Peterson rose from the desk and came towards them, hands outstretched. She looked crisply professional in a cream suit that had the hallmark of designer-label on it, and her grey hair was smoothed into a neat chignon.

The reserve she had shown at the interview in London had entirely dissipated, and there was a warmth in her eyes that made Joanne feel instantly less nervous. She clasped Joanne's hands and enquired anxiously, 'How are you this morning, my dear? Rested, I hope. And did you have enough breakfast?'

'Yes, thank you very much,' returned Joanne. 'And I'm feeling fine now. I slept very soundly.'

'Good! We shall take you along to the clinic shortly, but first I would like to talk to you about your duties.' The doctor exchanged a swift glance with her son which made Joanne feel apprehensive again.

Daniel evidently intended to stay for the interview, because after pushing up a comfortable armchair for Joanne, he sank into one himself and crossed one leg over his thigh, clasping his hands behind his head. Joanne would rather have been interviewed by his mother alone. She felt uneasy with him there, the more so because she was sitting side-on to him. He could watch her, but she could only see him out of the corner of her eye or by turning her head.

He said to his mother, 'You'd better tell her everything right away. She's already met Marie-Claire.'

Dr Ahlberg-Peterson directed a sharp look at her son and her lips compressed a little. She turned to Joanne. 'There were some aspects of the position which I did not discuss at your interview in London, Joanne. I hope you'll understand that this was because of the position's highly confidential nature. It wouldn't have been proper of me to acquaint every applicant with information that could lead to the invasion of privacy, were someone to be indiscreet.'

Joanne said, 'I see,' without properly seeing at all. She already knew that privacy was a high priority at the Harder-Kulm Clinic, but discretion was, or should be, second nature to a nurse, particularly perhaps a psychiatric nurse. She waited for the mystery to be explained.

'Your duties,' Dr Ahlberg-Peterson said, 'are to be two-fold.'

'How do you mean?' queried Joanne.

The Swiss woman's eyes clouded suddenly with an anxious expression. 'We have many patients at the clinic,' she explained, 'but we also have one here in this house.

Marie-Claire, my daughter, Daniel's sister. . .' A slight
catch in her voice made Joanne alert. That, plus her tense
encounter with the girl a short time previously.

'What's wrong with Marie-Claire?' she asked directly.

Daniel said, before his mother could answer, 'She was—
a bit antagonistic. She won't like it. . .'

A stubborn expression crossed his mother's face. They
probably had a lot in common temperamentally, Joanne
thought instantly, and doubtless they sometimes clashed.

Dr Ahlberg-Peterson said apologetically, 'I'm sorry,
Miss Courtney. I had hoped to explain to you about Marie-
Claire before you met her.' She paused and Joanne could
see that it was painful for her. She went on, 'I'll be brief. You
can ask any questions you may have later. Either Daniel or
I will answer you and we will of course give you our utmost
support. You asked what was wrong with Marie-Claire .'
She drew in a deep breath and in almost a whisper said,
'Her husband was killed in a racing car smash nearly a year
ago.'

'Paolo Valli!' Joanne was astonished. 'Le Mans—I
remember. . .'

'You're a racing-car fan?' As Daniel spoke, Joanne
glanced round and caught a faintly surprised look.

'No, not really. I just happened to catch it on television...'
She flinched inwardly at the memory of the terrible crash
that had killed the Italian world champion. 'It was very
tragic.' She also vaguely recalled newspaper photographs
of a distraught dark-haired young woman being
comforted at the scene of the accident.

'Marie-Claire's trauma is deep,' said the girl's mother,
her face showing a composure she clearly did not feel.

'Had she been treated in hospital?' asked Joanne.

'No. She's pathologically opposed to hospitalisation
and even medication of any kind. As she has deep-rooted
feelings of hostility towards us, her family, she behaves

often in a somewhat paranoid manner. She believes we're hostile towards her.'

For a moment Dr Ahlberg-Peterson's expression betrayed her extreme anxiety for her daughter, and she expressed feelings which moved Joanne deeply. 'Marie-Claire was such a beautiful, happy girl,' Daniel's mother said quietly. 'She was always so energetic, so outgoing, and so much in love with Paolo. He was not the playboy the press always liked to make him out to be, as we soon discovered. Not after he married Marie-Claire anyway. They had only one year together. She's only twenty. . .'

'Mama. . .' interposed Daniel gently.

Dr Ahlberg-Peterson immediately became businesslike again. 'We've asked you to live here with us in the house,' she said, 'as a kind of last straw, if I may say so without offending you. You're nearer Marie-Claire's age and you may be able to get through to her as anyone who's not a nurse could not be expected to do. I'm sure you appreciate the importance of establishing emotional rapport in cases like this and preventing emotional isolation.' Joanne nodded and the doctor went on, 'She's not to know why you are here, of course, or she might rebel against it, so you've also been engaged to work at the clinic, since we had a vacancy there anyway.'

'She's bound to be suspicious, surely,' Joanne suggested.

'Of course she will,' said Daniel rather tersely, his words directed at his mother. 'Just telling her there's no accommodation for the new nurse at the clinic won't convince her. She's suspicious of everything we do. Marie-Claire isn't a fool!'

His mother's eyes flashed with annoyance. 'It's true that we have no accommodation available,' she insisted.

Daniel said to Joanne, 'We have limited staff quarters at the clinic. Most of the staff live locally. And we certainly don't usually billet anyone here.'

Dr Ahlberg-Peterson said quietly, 'Daniel, I know it might not work. I know there might be problems—tantrums even—but we have to do something. We've tried everything...' For a moment Joanne was afraid her control would snap, as her voice wavered on a desperately pleading note.

Her distress obviously reached her son, for his face softened and he said, 'Yes, all right, Mama.'

She looked at Joanne. 'I hope you will appreciate that we may have to abandon the experiment, but of course that would make no difference to your job at the clinic.'

Daniel said, 'Perhaps Miss Courtney would prefer not to take on the task now it's been explained to her.' Looking directly at her, he added, 'You're under no obligation to do so.'

Joanne, who had turned to face him, searched his face carefully. Undoubtedly he was hoping she would change her mind. That was what a scatterbrain would probably do.

She met his gaze unflinchingly, and all at once it became of paramount importance to prove to him that she was not at all scatterbrained or stupid, that she was as capable as anyone of helping his sister. And she thought of Marie-Claire's sad empty gaze and knew that her hostility was a cry for help she had to try and answer.

'I quite understand why I was not told the complete story before,' she heard herself saying, 'and I'll be happy to try and help Marie-Claire as unobtrusively as I can.' Under Daniel's steely gaze she lifted her chin a shade defiantly. His mother gave a faint sigh of relief.

'We've managed to keep Marie-Claire sheltered from public gaze,' Dr Ahlberg-Peterson said, 'and naturally we wish to continue protecting her privacy. It will be the anniversary of Paolo's death in a few months and there's certain to be a renewed interest in his widow. She suffered greatly from exposure to the glare of publicity at the time of the accident, and if the press were to discover details of her breakdown I'm certain they would not hesitate to splash the story in a highly emotional way. You know that Paolo has become something of a cult figure amongst some young people?'

'Yes, I did read something about it,' Joanne acknowledged. 'And I understand the importance of privacy in a case like this. Even a sympathetic story, if she were to see it, could be regressive.'

Dr Ahlberg-Peterson nodded. 'We can't keep newspapers and magazines from her, naturally. She demands certain ones and she also watches a great deal of television.'

Joanne asked, 'Does she ever go out?'

Daniel answered. 'Never alone, and rarely with us. She hates going out. She's lost interest in everything.'

'She is subject to long periods of complete withdrawal,' his mother added. 'And we hope, Miss Courtney, that you may be able to do what we cannot. She may respond to you, a stranger, far more easily than to us, her family.' She glanced at her son, then back at Joanne, 'It's a matter of seeing how things turn out. That is, if you're willing to give it a try?' She still seemed doubtful, in spite of what Joanne had said.

Joanne could see that the strain of Marie-Claire's illness had taken its toll of both of them. She said firmly, 'I'll do my best.'

'Thank you,' Daniel's mother said gratefully, and smiled at her son as though inviting him to confirm that her choice had been a good one after all. But his expression did not yield. She went on, 'There's no need for us to be formal at home—we use first names at the clinic for convenience most of the time—so I hope you will allow me to call you Joanne, and I would like you to call me Luise. I'm sure

Daniel will have no objection to your using his name either.'

Daniel merely nodded. He rose abruptly. 'Shall we take Joanne to the clinic now?'

His mother also rose. 'Unfortunately, I have to go to Lucerne this morning, and I'm running a little late already, so would you mind taking Joanne, Daniel? You can hand her over to Esther.' She said to Joanne, 'Sister Madigan is my right hand, and she'll show you the ropes and help you to settle in.'

They all moved to the door and when Daniel had hurried away to fetch the car around, Luise turned to Joanne and gripped her wrists. 'Don't worry that Daniel is a little opposed to your being here. He's only anxious for Marie-Claire. But I'm convinced it's the right thing to do, and I'm so glad you're going to stay with us.'

It was certainly far from the situation she had expected, Joanne thought as she ran upstairs to collect her handbag and warm jacket. Her misgivings about the job were even deeper now, but it was too late to change her mind. All she could hope for was that by her actions, she could soon make Daniel see her in a more favourable light.

He drove her to the clinic, which was a mere five minutes away, situated in large grounds sweeping down to the lake which Joanne had glimpsed from her bedroom window that morning and which, Daniel had since told her, was Lake Thun.

The clinic was more like a luxury hotel than a hospital. There were no wards as such, only rooms and suites and communal areas such as games rooms, lounges and writing and reading rooms.

To the casual observer it might even have seemed there were no doctors or nurses, since they dressed in everyday clothes like the patients. Only not as expensively, Joanne thought, comparing her chain-store outfit with one or two of the couturier dresses she saw when Daniel showed her around and introduced her to both staff and patients as they encountered them.

She had been expected to be handed straight over to Sister Madigan, but the charge nurse was busy when they arrived and so Daniel gallantly offered to show her around himself.

'The grounds are particularly beautiful in spring and summer,' he told her, when they were standing at a large picture window looking towards the lake. Did he expect her still to be there then? Joanne wondered wryly. She had a contract for a year, but she sensed he would find a way to break it if he wanted to.

As they turned from the window a tall, rather voluptuous woman approached. Her silver hair was done in an elaborate style, but she was not old, probably no more than forty.

She spoke rapidly in German to Daniel, who smiled and nodded and when he could get a word in edgewise, managed to say, 'Countess, I would like you to meet our new nurse, Joanne Courtney from England.'

A heavily beringed hand took Joanne's in a shaky grasp. 'I have happy memories of London—very happy memories.' She sighed theatrically.

As she spoke a traymobile was wheeled into the room and the aroma of freshly brewed coffee was pungent on the air.

'Ah, coffee!' said Daniel, with a glance at Joanne. 'Shall we go to my office? Then you can ask any questions you've thought of while we have ours.'

He politely excused them, and they went, Daniel acknowledging on the way a number of other patients who were gathering for morning coffee in the lounge. In his

office, which was restfully decorated in shades of cream
and brown with touches of pale and dark green, and a
couple of Paul Klee paintings on the walls, Daniel waved
Joanne into a chair and said, 'The Countess is an alcoholic,
but perhaps you guessed as much?'

'It did cross my mind.'

'This is her third visit here. I hope this time we can effect
a permanent cure. She used to be an opera singer. I
wondered if you recognised her.'

'Her face did seem vaguely familiar, but I couldn't have
said why. I like opera, but I don't often go. I used to go with
my father now and then.'

He smiled indulgently and told her the singer's name.
'She really is a countess. Occasionally a client goes by a
pseudonym, but usually only in very special
circumstances. We've found sticking to first names the best
way, and it's rare for anyone to object.'

The morning tea trolley arrived, and after they had been
served coffee and biscuits, Daniel pressed a number on his
internal phone. 'I'll ask our resident psychiatrist to come
and have coffee with us if he's free.' He returned briefly to
their previous conversation after he had put the phone
down. 'Alcohol did not prove the booster to a waning
career that the Countess hoped.'

'Does it ever?' commented Joanne, and he nodded.

The door flew open and a tall fair-haired man in a tweed
sports jacket with leather patched elbows breezed in.
Daniel introduced him.

'This is Doctor Schmid—Bernard.'

Dr Schmid bowed low over Joanne's hand. '*Meine
Fräulein*, I am enchanted!' His eyes flirted with her and she
glimpsed in their blue depths a twinkling humour.

'I've been showing Joanne over the clinic,' said Daniel, in
a slightly clipped tone as though he did not approve of
Bernard's familiarity. 'Naturally I haven't yet had time to

discuss any of our clients with her. I shall leave that to you and Esther. See that she has all the case notes to study, won't you, Bernard.'

'I shall enjoy the task immensely,' said Bernard gallantly. He added with interest, 'What brings you to Switzerland to work, Joanne?'

'I've always wanted to work abroad, but until my widowed father married again recently, I hadn't the opportunity. Besides, I love skiing!'

'I'm glad to hear that,' said Bernard. 'We shall certainly see that you get your fair ration. Eh, Daniel?'

Daniel made a noncommittal sound and asked, 'How is Anna, Bernard?'

The young psychiatrist dragged his attention reluctantly away from Joanne. 'Anna? She's responding well to the reduced doses you recommended. But she's still showing signs of tardive dyskinesia, I'm afraid. I'm hopeful that problem will disappear in time.'

The two men continued to converse on the subject of the side effects of some neuroleptic drugs and Joanne listened attentively, trying to pick up what information she could about the patient Anna, who was apparently suffering from the involuntary muscular movements, which could be an unpleasant side-effect of prolonged use of some drugs. Finally the two men remembered she was there, and Bernard apologised.

Joanne said, 'That's all right. I was most interested in the discussion.'

Bernard left them then, and a few minutes later Daniel handed Joanne over to Esther Madigan who, to Joanne's relief, also spoke excellent English. She had worked in British hospitals for several years and was now married and lived locally. Her husband was the manager of a *Gasthof* in one of the ski-resort villages.

'You won't have any language problems here,' Esther

assured Joanne. 'We use English as our common language. Most of the staff speak it and so do most of the clients.'

'I want to improve my German, though,' said Joanne hopefully.

'You will,' Esther assured her. 'You'll probably brush up your French too, and pick up a sprinkling of Spanish, Italian and any other language you fancy. We're very cosmopolitan!' She gave a laugh. 'We usually have quite a few rich Americans staying here, and English people too. Since they rarely speak any other language, we have to speak English. They're paying!'

She gave Joanne a brief résumé of the histories of most of the current resident clients.

'We don't call them patients,' she explained, and outlined the conditions Joanne was likely to encounter, from alcoholism to anorexia nervosa and various types of depression.

'We have a few permanent residents,' she told her, 'most of whom are rather old. Most of our clients get better and go home. Some come back, unfortunately, but we're proud of our successes here. Harder-Kulm psychotherapy is reputedly amongst the best in the world. Dr Peterson is highly respected.' With a sly glance, she added, 'What do you think of him?'

The question took Joanne by surprise. 'I—I only met him last night. He seems very nice.' It sounded so fatuous. Intimidating would have been a more honest description.

Esther laughed as she tucked a stray strand of red hair behind her ear. 'It usually takes less time than that for a new nurse to fall head over heels in love with Dr Peterson,' she said dryly. 'Not to mention a few of our glamorous and not so glamorous clients. Daniel has oodles of sex appeal. Surely you must have noticed!'

'I was too tired last night to notice anything!' Joanne told her, but that wasn't strictly true. Daniel had had a rather disturbing effect on her, which she wasn't ready to admit even to herself.

Esther said curiously, 'Then you must have a very handsome boyfriend back home!'

'No, not really,' Joanne said too soberly.

'Ah—is it that you don't know exactly how you stand with him?' Esther probed.

'You're very perceptive!'

'That's what we're trained to be, isn't it?' said Esther.

Joanne conceded, 'Well, you're half right.' It was a relief to talk about Luke, which she hadn't been able to do at the Barmouth, so she told Esther a little about him.

Esther was sympathetic. 'I think you did the right thing, Joanne. It would have been foolish to chase after him. Now, if he comes back and expects to find you waiting around for him, he'll get a shock.' She laughed. 'Maybe he'll come hotfeeting it over here to find you!'

'Hotfooting!'

They both laughed and Joanne had the feeling that she and Esther were going to be friends.

The buzzer sounded on Esther's desk and she answered it. '*Ja*, Gerda—*danke*.' She turned to Joanne. 'We've got a routine ECT treatment shortly. Would you like to watch? The client is one of Daniel's. Daniel's not wild about ECT, but it does seem to benefit some people, and Geoffrey is responding very satisfactorily.'

On the way to the treatment room, Esther explained that Geoffrey was a company executive suffering work-related stress problems as well as difficulties in his personal life, and he became severely depressed from time to time. For him, a course of ECT had beneficial effects for quite a long duration.

'He's a workaholic,' Esther told Joanne. 'And I wonder just how long he can go on the way he is doing. There are early signs of heart disease, and he's only forty-three. Why

do people drive themselves so hard?' she finished
reflectively.

Daniel, looking different in a white coat, nodded
formally at Joanne when she entered with Esther. He
introduced her to the anaesthetist, Alain Lagrange, and
Esther introduced the other nurse present as Gerda
Volker. Joanne sensed a strong feeling of resentment from
the girl, despite her pleasant enough greeting. She hoped
she was just being hypersensitive.

Joanne had met the patient, Geoffrey, earlier and he
asked now how she was settling in. He was used to the
routine of electro-convulsive therapy, so no preliminary
reassurances were needed and the treatment began as
soon as the anaesthetist was ready.

Alain glanced at Gerda, saying, 'Geoffrey's had pre-
med atropine?'

She sounded sullen as she replied, 'Yes, of course, the
exact dose you ordered.'

His eyes narrowed slightly, but he said patiently, 'Just
checking.'

Something's bugging her, Joanne thought, and she's
taking it out on everyone.

Joanne remained a little apart while the patient was
prepared, as she was anxious not to be intrusive. She
noticed that the preferred treatment was apparently the
unilateral method, with both electrodes being placed on
the same side of the patient's head. This method was
favoured at the Barmouth too, because of less
troublesome after-effects. The bilateral method was
usually only used when rapid initial improvement was
urgently required. Geoffrey would be less confused
afterwards this way, and might not even have a headache.

For a few moments Joanne's attention was on the
patient, and then she found herself studying Daniel's
profile with concentration, and annoyingly thinking of

what Esther had said about him earlier.

He was handsome, no doubt about that, and there was certainly an element of sex appeal in his well-defined features, especially his eyes with their dark lashes. His movements had a powerful, precise character, and Joanne found herself thinking that he would have made a good surgeon. And with that kind of control he was probably an expert skier, she thought.

Then all at once her thoughts were out of control and she was thinking, for a wayward moment, how it would feel to have her arms around him and to be tightly enfolded in his. Disconcertingly, her heartbeat was suddenly taking off as though she'd entered a sprint.

The indoor temperature was warmer than she was accustomed to and although she was standing very still so as to be unobtrusive, neither factor should have precipitated what happened next. Suddenly the room began to sway and without warning she slid into a heap on the floor.

She didn't hear Daniel's surprised and urgent, 'Good God, the girl's fainted!' She only heard his words as she was coming round seconds later, 'What a damn fool thing to do! Surely she's seen a patient in a fit before!'

A wave of humiliation swept over her. A nurse who fainted during any kind of operation or treatment was the last gasp. Only raw students did that!

CHAPTER THREE

'STOP worrying!' said Sister Madigan. 'It was nothing.'

Joanne was sipping a cup of tea in Esther's office. 'I've never fainted before—not on duty,' she groaned, thoroughly disgusted with herself. 'I felt such a fool. After all, I hadn't been standing up all that long. It was a bit warm, though.'

Esther said, 'We do have our central heating a little higher than you're probably accustomed to. And everything is new and strange for you. It was quite natural really, nothing to worry about.'

She was being kind, but Joanne still felt a fool. 'But right in the middle of a treatment! If I'd been trying to make a bad impression, I couldn't have done worse,' she said gloomily. 'Daniel will think I'm very unreliable.'

Esther laughed. 'Nonsense! He was very sympathetic. He picked you up and laid you on the other couch as tenderly as though you were a child. He was very concerned. Lucky you! Gerda would give anything to get so close!'

Remembering that she had been thinking about being in Daniel's arms only moments before she fainted made Joanne colour faintly. However, despite what Esther had said, she was sure Daniel must be extremely displeased with her, and she dreaded facing him again.

'I suggest you spend the rest of the day quietly reading case notes,' Esther suggested.

'To keep me out of mischief?' said Joanne with a grin, and they laughed together.

Presently, when Gerda came in with a message for Esther, the senior nurse glanced at her watch and asked her to take Joanne to lunch.

'Are you feeling better?' asked Gerda as they went out together. Her enquiry was more polite than concerned and she gave Joanne a carefully appraising look.

'Yes, thanks. I don't know what came over me.'

'Maybe it was Dr Peterson,' said Gerda, without appearing to be joking.

'Do you think so?' Joanne replied, feigning seriousness. 'Does it happen often?'

Gerda shot her a rather perplexed look, not understanding the irony. She shrugged a little huffily and pushed open the door to the staff dining room. Joanne felt ill at ease with her and hoped they were not going to clash.

Joanne was warmly greeted by other members of the staff she had not so far met, and the atmosphere was very friendly and welcoming. She was relieved to find that Daniel was not present; an overheard snatch of conversation told her that he had left a short time ago.

She and Gerda sat at an empty table and Joanne attempted to make friendly conversation with the girl, but Gerda seemed in no mood for small talk and answered mostly in monosyllables. It was a relief when they were joined a few minutes later by Bernard Schmid. Gerda's face lit up at once, but her mouth tightened when Bernard elected to sit next to Joanne, and, practically ignoring Gerda, asked her when she had last been skiing.

'More than a year ago,' she replied. 'I'm a bit rusty.'

'Rusty?' queried Gerda, who perhaps resented the conversation being in English. 'What is that?'

'Out of practice,' laughed Joanne.

Bernard said, 'That means we must go skiing at the first opportunity. When is your day off?'

'I've no idea! I haven't thought about days off yet,'

Joanne told him. 'This is only my first day at work!'

'I'll fix it so that we have a day off together,' said Bernard, 'and we'll go up the Schilthorn. Piz Gloria is my favourite place.'

Joanne wished he hadn't made the arrangement in front of Gerda, but it crossed her mind that perhaps he had done so deliberately. When Bernard's bleeper interrupted, he hastily departed, leaving the two girls to finish their coffee.

Gerda said, a trifle sarcastically, 'Well, at least he didn't make you faint!'

Joanne could not resist a grin. 'Willpower, Gerda, that's all that saved me!' She did not want to tease the girl, but she knew she would have to keep it light or she might be tempted some time into a sharp retort.

News of Bernard's invitation reached Esther before Joanne did. 'So Bernard's going to take you skiing,' she remarked, lifting her eyebrows slightly.

'Did he tell you?'

'Yes.' Esther hesitated, then added, 'It's not my business, but—be careful, Joanne. Don't let Bernard go to your head—or your heart. He's not the marrying kind, as Gerda is learning and one or two others in the past have found out. I suspect a past disappointment which has embittered him, so he hides his true feelings under a flirtatious facade.'

'I thought Gerda looked displeased when he arranged to go skiing with me,' Joanne said, her suspicions now confirmed.

Esther shrugged. 'It was probably sensible of him. Gerda is a rather intense girl. She seems to fall madly in love with every doctor who shows his nose in the place, and she flirts with patients too! She has some high and mighty notions of making a good catch.' She laughed. 'Gerda's always moaning because she has no money. She's looking for someone to keep her in the manner to which she would like to become accustomed!' She added, 'Don't let Gerda goad you. She may not be with us much longer in any case. In my opinion she's not suitable material for psychiatric nursing.' Esther smiled and changed the subject. 'Would you like to help me do the afternoon medications? Do you feel up to it?'

'Heavens, yes! I only fainted, you know! I feel much better since I had lunch. Maybe that was part of the trouble—now I come to think of it, I didn't eat much yesterday and I rushed breakfast this morning, trying to make a good impression by not dawdling.'

After visiting each patient, most of whom were in their private rooms, Esther offered brief explanations.

'Marianne is a lovely person,' she said after they had spent a few very pleasant minutes with a French girl who was a well-known model and whose face had appeared on the covers of countless fashion magazines. 'She's not a bit affected or demanding, and not as brittle as you might expect.'

Marianne had taken an overdose of sleeping pills and after a short time in hospital, had come to the clinic to recuperate.

'I doubt if she did it on purpose,' Esther reflected. 'She was just overwrought. She's a bit of a hypochondriac. You should have seen the boxes of pills she brought with her! Mostly what we call "alternative" medicine. Daniel confiscated the lot. Not that there was any harm in them, but none were treating her real problems. He insisted that she have a thorough medical check and then gave her some medication with a very fancy name. She doesn't know it's a name he made up for an ordinary placebo! It's the psychotherapy that's really doing her good.'

'What's her main problem?' asked Joanne.

'Fear. She's terrified of getting sick and losing work. There are plenty of up-and-coming models just dying to slip into her shoes. She's nearly thirty, and the going gets tougher the older you get. I just hope she doesn't check herself out of here too soon because she's afraid of being forgotten.'

For a very tall, much too thin girl, Esther was even more anxious. 'Elsa is anorexic, as you probably realised. She's a difficult case. Her chief problem seems to be a very talented older sister who is a musician. Elsa feels she has no talent for anything and therefore is not worthwhile. The only thing she can be proud of is being ultra-slim. Like all anorexics, she doesn't see herself as an ugly skeleton.'

Amongst the men was one with whom Esther seemed to have a special rapport. Inevitably nurses related better to some patients than others, and you could always help a mentally ill person more effectively, Joanne knew, if you had real empathy with them.

Johannes was a tall, stooped man with dark hair greying at the temples and an attractive, rather wistful smile. He put down the newspaper he was reading and greeted the two women warmly.

'How's the stock market today, Johannes?' asked Esther.

In a low, confidential voice he answered, 'There will be a big fall, Sister, mark my words. You would be wise to sell some stocks right now—put your money in gold or real estate.' He stabbed his finger at the newspaper crumpled on his knees. 'Economists! Fools! They don't know what they are talking about. The crunch is coming!'

Later, Esther told Joanne, 'He had a complete collapse three months ago. He was managing director of a company that crashed and he got the blame for it. He's a real gentleman. I feel so sorry for his wife. She's very charming and obviously very much in love with him.'

Joanne commented, 'Work-related stress seems to be a big problem everywhere nowadays. The more high-tech our society becomes the less people seem to be able to cope with it.'

'Unfortunately, yes. Business is waking up to it at long last, though, and there are many excellent staff programmes that try to tackle stress before it reaches the stage of breakdown. If people would only realise how long it takes to recover from a nervous breakdown they might take more care not to push themselves too far. Sometimes I fear for Jurgen, my husband. He works all hours at the *Gasthof*, but will he listen to me when I say, ease up? Of course not!'

Almost before Joanne realised it, her first day's work was finished. Already she was becoming familiar with the patients, the clinic's routines and the staff. Even the morning's unfortunate incident was diminished in her mind because everyone had been friendly and helpful and had made her feel that she already belonged.

Esther was going off duty at the same time as Joanne, and as they were preparing to hand over to the evening shift, she said, 'Well, how do you feel now? The first day is always the worst in a new job, isn't it?'

Joanne nodded. 'I was a bit nervous this morning, I suppose, but I've enjoyed my day. Everything is a little different from what I've been used to, but I expected that. And it's good to have a change. I was in a rut at the Barmouth.'

Esther considered her kindly. 'I don't mind telling you, Joanne, I'm always a little bit nervous when a new nurse arrives. Our isn't the easiest kind of nursing, despite what some people think. But I can see you're going to fit in splendidly. I'm glad to have you on the team.'

Joanne was warmed by the compliment. 'Thanks.'

'Now, how are you getting home? Did Daniel say he'd be back for you?'

'No, he didn't. I'd better get a taxi.'

'I certainly won't let you do that,' Esther insisted. 'I'll

drive you. It's not far out of my way.' She lowered her voice slightly. 'I'm not going to say much about it because it's none of my business, but I know why you're living at the Ahlberg-Peterson place. Some of the staff have probably guessed too. I just want to say that if ever you need to talk about Marie-Claire and you don't want to talk to Daniel or Luise, you'll find a sympathetic ear in this office, or in Bernard's. Nothing you say will go any further.'

'Thank you,' said Joanne, touched. 'I'll remember that.'

A few minutes later as they were donning their coats ready to leave, Daniel pushed open the door. He riveted Joanne with a steely look.

'If you're ready, we can go now.'

Joanne's pulse quickened involuntarily and she quaked a little inside. Would he vent his wrath on her for her foolishness that morning, once they were alone? She dreaded the inevitable confrontation.

'Oh, you're back, Daniel,' said Esther, 'I was just going to run Joanne home.'

He smiled at her. 'Kind of you, Esther, but I'll take care of her now.'

'I'll be off, then,' said Esther. *'Auf Wiedersehen.'*

Daniel did not say much on the way home and he made no reference to the morning's incident. Joanne, however, remained in a state of apprehension, certain he would upbraid her when they reached the house.

'Did you have a good day?' he asked a trifle brusquely.

'Yes, thank you. Everyone was very friendly and helpful.'

'I'm pleased to hear it.'

He was being impeccably polite, and Joanne felt guilty because she was sure he didn't really want to be. Not to her. She was too overawed by him to try to make conversation herself and therefore made only brief answers when he spoke to her, which was only two or three times.

It was already nearly dark when they reached the house, and the cloud had crept down low over the mountain peaks.

'We shall have more snow tonight,' remarked Daniel, as they went indoors together and he held the door open for her. He added, 'We have dinner about eight. Do join us for an aperitif beforehand, in the drawing room.' He indicated a door off the hall and then politely excused himself. Or dismissed her, Joanne thought.

When Joanne came downstairs just before eight o'clock, she heard voices in the drawing-room and rather nervously paused with her hand on the doorknob before going in.

'Please come in, Joanne,' said a voice behind her suddenly. 'They won't bite you!'

Joanne wheeled round to find Marie-Claire regarding her with the same flat expression as that morning. She was wearing the same sloppy sweater and jeans. Her face was devoid of make-up, but her hair was clean and shining. She had not completely let herself go, which was encouraging.

'*Guten Abend*, Marie-Claire,' murmured Joanne, but the girl did not bother to respond. As Joanne opened the door, Daniel was speaking, but the conversation ceased abruptly as the two girls came in. Joanne, however, caught Daniel's last words: '. . .right in the middle of an ECT treatment this morning!' She cringed inside.

Daniel was standing near the crackling log fire in the enormous grate and he fixed her with a steady gaze. His mother greeted them warmly.

'Joanne—Marie-Claire—*guten Abend*.'

Joanne felt a little hesitant about joining this family gathering and she was surprised when Daniel came forward and touched her arm. 'Come closer to the fire. Would you like a drink? We have sherry, brandy, whisky— or perhaps you have a liking for schnapps?' His eyes twinkled as though he was mocking her.

'I'd like a sherry, please,' said Joanne, and was very much aware of his observant eyes taking in and approving the figure-hugging but demure black skivvy and dark green velvet skirt and waistcoat she had changed into.

Marie-Claire had sunk morosely into a chair and was staring into the fire. She seemed to have forgotten the rest of them were even there. Daniel queried whether she would like a drink, but she did not answer. He did not press her.

Luise Ahlberg-Peterson looked Joanne over too as she sat down near her. 'Daniel has just been telling me,' she said, 'how quickly you have fitted into the clinic.'

How tactful! Joanne thought; she doesn't know, of course, that I overheard enough to guess what he had really been saying. She said, 'I'm sure I shall enjoy working there.'

'I'm sorry I wasn't able to be there myself today,' Luise apologised.

Marie-Claire turned suddenly and said, 'I'm sure Joanne much preferred the attentions of Daniel!'

Joanne accepted the sherry Daniel handed her and forced herself to reply smilingly, 'Actually I spent most of the day with Sister Madigan. Doctor Schmid was also very helpful.' She did not dare look at Daniel.

It was Luise who adroitly released the tension that Marie-Claire's remark evoked.

'When we talked in London, you mentioned that your father is a civil engineer,' she said conversationally. 'Does his work ever take him abroad?'

'Not now,' answered Joanne. 'My mother and he were often away for a year or more at a time, and I lived with my grandmother for most of my childhood, but after Mother died, Dad stopped going away. I kept house for him until he got married again quite recently. He and Terri, his new wife, flew off to the Caribbean for a belated honeymoon cruise only a few days before I came here. . .' She slowed down, fearing she was boring them.

'The Caribbean,' murmured Daniel. 'How I envy them!'

He's bored, thought Joanne, nettled by his supercilious look and wishing he would direct his gaze somewhere other than at her. Like many other psychiatrists she knew, he had a way of looking at people who weren't even patients, as though he was reading their minds. It was very disconcerting, and for some reason made her very much aware of his undeniably masculine good looks.

When Fräulein Müller announced dinner, they went through double doors to the dining room. On the walls were several large oil paintings which caught Joanne's eye immediately.

'I was admiring the paintings on the stairs this morning,' she said. 'Are these by the same artist?'

Luise looked pleased with her interest. 'Yes, indeed!' She rested her hand lightly on her daughter's shoulder. 'Marie-Claire is the artist in the family.'

'The colours are wonderful,' said Joanne, going closer to examine one of the canvases. 'So vibrant and—joyous.' She glanced at the girl, who stood impassively, making no response. 'You're very talented, Marie-Claire. Are you painting anything at the moment?'

'No.' Marie-Claire's tone very clearly indicated that she did not wish to discuss painting.

Joanne caught a warning glance from Daniel and did not pursue the subject.

After dinner, Marie-Claire vanished. Between the dining room and the drawing room she just slipped away without Joanne even noticing.

'She'll have coffee in her room,' said Daniel. 'I'm afraid she's very unpredictable and not very sociable.'

'Tonight is the first time this week she has come down for

dinner,' Luise put in. 'Her curiosity about you, Joanne, must have got the better of her. But oh dear, still in that awful sweater and old jeans! And she has so many beautiful clothes.'

Daniel lifted the decanter from the silver tray on the side table and looked enquiringly at Joanne. 'Would you care for Kirsch with your coffee?'

Joanne accepted, and as he poured the liqueur into a tiny crystal glass, ventured, 'It might help a lot if Marie-Claire could become interested in painting again.'

Luise shrugged. 'She hasn't picked up a brush since the accident. She has lost interest in everything. The creative urge seems quite dead.'

During the next few minutes, Joanne asked a few more questions about Marie-Claire so as to build up a more complete picture, and she tried to read a little between the lines too.

Presently Luise invited her to watch television, but Joanne declined, saying she was rather tired and thought she would rather go to bed early. This was true, but she also did not want to appear to be making herself at home too readily.

'You've had a hectic time this past two days,' Luise agreed, and added, 'You'll find everything you need in your room should you want to make yourself a bedtime drink.'

Joanne murmured goodnight, and as she left them she felt Daniel's gaze boring into her back.

'I'm sure you're wrong, Daniel,' said Luise as the door closed behind Joanne. 'She seems to me to be a very intelligent and well-adjusted young woman. Compassionate too. Marie-Claire may well respond to her.'

Daniel poured out more coffee. 'I concede that I may have to eat my words,' he said with a smile. 'Appearances can be deceptive.'

It would have warmed Joanne's heart to hear what he had said, but she had fled too swiftly to catch a word of it.

She reached her room with a sigh of relief and closed the door. The past couple of hours had been something of a strain as she had been half expecting all evening that Daniel would take her to task for her unprofessional behaviour that morning. Now at last she could relax.

She undressed and got ready for bed, then sat on the edge of it to write in her diary. After that she planned to relax for an hour with the paperback novel she had bought to read on the journey and had not even opened. And after that maybe she would indulge in the luxury of making herself a hot bedtime drink. The tray on her table contained an electric kettle, packets of chocolate, coffee and tea and a small jug of milk.

'What luxury!' she exclaimed, stretching her toes before she tucked them under her and began to record the events of the day and her impressions in her diary.

She was deeply absorbed when there was a perfunctory knock on the door. Before she had time to call, 'Come in!' the door swung open and Marie-Claire walked in. She was also in night attire. She had drawn her dark hair back and secured it with a band and the effect was to make her seem very young and vulnerable. There was so much suffering locked up behind those pretty grey-blue eyes and the rigidity of her features that Joanne's heart ached for her.

'Why, hello, Marie-Claire!' she exclaimed, pleased that the girl had come of her own accord. 'Won't you sit down?'

Marie-Claire remained standing. 'Daniel has had scores of girlfriends,' she said unexpectedly.

'I'm not surprised,' said Joanne levelly. 'He's a good-looking man.'

'Are you his new mistress?' snapped Marie-Claire.

The shock question made Joanne's cheeks flame.

'Heavens, no!' she answered, and laughed. 'Goodness, I only met him yesterday! I'm not here because of Daniel, Marie-Claire. It's only because there's no accommodation at the clinic.'

Marie-Claire scoffed, 'They could have billeted you somewhere else. Daniel wants you here, obviously.'

'I'm sure he's never given it a thought,' said Joanne.

'You'll see!' Marie-Claire said with a laugh. 'Daniel always gets his own way. He rules! Everyone. Do you know that in the past few months he's brought—oh, a dozen different girls home. It means nothing to him. None of them last long. He'll never commit himself again unless it's to Elise. She might be fool enough to have him—he sees a lot of her when she isn't dancing. She's a ballet dancer.' She paused briefly, then said, 'He was married once, you know.'

'No, I didn't know.'

'It was a total disaster.'

'They're divorced?'

Marie-Claire stared hard at Joanne. 'She died. Poor Ingrid.' Tears suddenly welled up and ran down her cheeks, but her expression scarcely changed. 'I'm such a tiresome burden to everyone. I might as well be dead too,' she whispered bitterly. 'There's no point in living without love.'

Her shoulders were shaking now, and Joanne quietly rose and went to her. She put her arm gently around the girl's shoulders and steered her out of the room and back to her own bedroom which was next door.

It was a soft, feminine room with a more modern decor than the rest of the house. A couple of Marie-Claire's own pictures hung on one wall, but what caught Joanne's eye was the large framed photograph of a smiling young man with handsome Italian features. She needed no one to tell her that this was Paolo Valli.

Marie-Claire did not resist when Joanne suggested she

get into bed. With a lace handkerchief that was on the bedside table, she wiped the tears from Marie-Claire's face and then said brightly, 'I'm going to make myself a hot drink before I go to bed. Would you like one too?'

Marie-Claire seemed for a moment not to have registered what she had said, then her eyes blinked and she turned her head and pointed across the room. She also had facilities for making hot drinks, Joanne saw.

'*Schokolade?*' Joanne asked, going over to the tray.

'*Danke,*' answered Marie-Claire rigidly.

Joanne switched on the kettle and ran into her own room to fetch her cup and saucer. When she returned, Marie-Claire was sobbing into the pillows. Joanne hesitated for a moment, then resolutely continued to make the hot drinks. By the time she placed both cups on the bedside table, Marie-Claire's storm of weeping had subsided.

'Marie-Claire, here's your hot chocolate,' Joanne coaxed, touching the girl's shoulder. She sat on the edge of the bed and gently prised Marie-Claire's clutching fingers from the pillow. The girl struggled and uttered a torrent of German which Joanne could not understand. Patiently she patted her shoulder and waited.

All at once Marie-Claire turned her head and seemed astonished to see Joanne.

'Your drink's getting cold,' Joanne said. 'I hate cold chocolate, don't you? My father's dog used to sit up and beg for the skins off hot milky drinks. He liked the ones off cocoa best. He was a cocker spaniel and we had him for years and years...' She hesitated slightly and Marie-Claire unexpectedly asked:

'What happened to it?'

Now Joanne wished she hadn't mentioned old Rags, but she told the truth. 'He died of old age.'

Tears filled Marie-Claire's eyes again. 'Poor dog,' she

whispered, and suddenly flung her arms around Joanne and sobbed on her shoulder. After a few moments she flopped back on her pillows and whispered urgently, 'Don't tell Daniel! Please don't tell Daniel! He'll make me go to hospital.'

'There's nothing to tell him,' Joanne assured her, smoothing the dark damp hair back from the girl's pale anguished face. 'Come on, have your drink.'

Marie-Claire accepted the cup with trembling fingers and sipped it. Joanne drank hers without speaking. Marie-Claire finished first and handed back the cup.

'Thank you.' She managed a very faint smile.

Joanne said, 'I suppose you're so used to it you don't realise how delicious real Swiss chocolate is to someone who hardly ever tastes it! If I don't watch out I'll become very fat!'

The smile hovered around Marie-Claires's mouth. 'You're very slim. You'll never be fat.'

'Perhaps not if I go skiing often,' said Joanne. 'You ski, of course, Marie Claire?'

The girl shook her head. 'Not now.' Her gaze became distant. She would have skied with Paolo, of course, Joanne thought. Somehow she had to help Marie-Claire find the courage to do again all the things she had done with Paolo.

'Dr Schmid is going to take me skiing soon,' said Joanne, carefully casual. 'Just say if you'd like to come with us.'

Marie-Claire looked terrified and shook her head. 'Oh, no. . .no, I never go out.'

Joanne did not press it. 'Well, just let me know if you change your mind. I'm sure Bernard would be delighted to take us both. I've heard he's a bit of a flirt, so I'd feel safer with company.'

Marie-Claire's smile almost came again, but the glazed look was still in her eyes as she closed them. Joanne picked up the cups and rinsed them in the bathroom, then seeing that Marie-Claire was now asleep, she put out the light and returned to her own room.

As she left Marie-Claire's room, Daniel was coming along the passage. He glanced at the cup and saucer in her hand. 'I thought you'd gone to bed.'

Joanne felt furtive and her voice shook as she said, 'I've been with Marie-Claire.'

He frowned suspiciously. 'Is something wrong? Did she have a nightmare?' There was apology and concern in his tone. 'Why didn't you call me?'

Not wanting to deceive him too blatantly, Joanne said, 'There was no need. She was a little upset, that's all. We had a cup of hot chocolate and a chat, and she's sleeping now.'

He eyed her sharply. It would never be easy to fool this highly perceptive man, Joanne thought.

'Weren't you rushing her a bit, trying to make contact so soon?' he asked, a trifle accusingly.

Joanne steeled herself. 'Marie-Claire came into my room.'

His eyebrows rose slightly. 'What happened?'

Joanne made a decision. 'I think it would be better, Daniel, if we didn't discuss my relationship with Marie-Claire. I want to be able to tell her truthfully that I haven't discussed her with you or anyone, if she asks. It's essential that she trusts me and talks to me, and she won't if she thinks I'm running to you behind her back. I'm sure she already guesses I'm here to watch her and report to you. Naturally I promise to report anything medically significant that I feel you should know.'

She met his gaze levelly, aware that she was acting in what in hospital terms could be called an insubordinate way, but her better judgement told her that she was right to take this attitude in this particular case. This was not a hospital or clinic situation.

Daniel's frown had deepened as she was talking and she was afraid he would now give her an angry dressing-down and tell her that he made the rules and she was being paid to obey them, but after a moment the corners of his mouth softened and gradually his lips parted in a smile that was grudgingly accepting. 'Whatever you feel is best.'

'Thank you.' Joanne was relieved. 'Just one question. If Marie-Claire wants to go out, may I take her—skiing, for instance? Or maybe shopping. There isn't much risk of her being recognised, is there?'

Daniel's dark grey-blue eyes weighed her up thoroughly. 'She won't go out. She hasn't set foot outside this house for months. There's no reason why she shouldn't, however, but I would advise against trying to persuade her to. She's sees persuasion as a threat.'

'I realise that. I won't pressure her to do anything, I just wanted to know the guidelines. Is there anything else I should know?'

He shook his head. 'No. But I must warn you—she rejects everyone. She hates us all because we're alive and Paolo isn't.' The pain in his eyes sent a surge of sympathy through Joanne.

'Yes, I understand that.' With her free hand she pulled her dressing-gown around her. 'I'd better go to bed.'

He detained her. 'By the way, there's a car in the garage you may use if you wish. The Fiat is Marie-Claire's.'

'Thank you—I'll ask her. . .'

'No, don't do that,' cautioned Daniel. 'She may be obstructive.' His eyes roved searchingly over her face. 'It seems you may have got closer to her than anyone else has done for a long time tonight.' He smiled faintly. 'Perhaps my mother was right and engaging a nurse was the right thing to do after all. Goodnight, Joanne.'

Joanne was almost too stunned by this unexpected admission to speak.

'Goodnight, Daniel,' she said, and was gripped with an intense desire to wipe the burden of anxiety from his face for ever. It was clear from his expression that Marie-Claire was wrong in thinking she was a tiresome burden; in fact she was a much loved responsibility.

CHAPTER FOUR

JOANNE was delighted to have the use of a car. She would have preferred to have asked Marie-Claire's permission first, as she felt it was important to be totally honest with her, but since Daniel had said not to, she had not gone against his wishes.

It was a relief when Marie-Claire brought the subject up only a few days later.

'You can use my car if you like, Joanne,' Marie-Claire offered one evening at dinner. 'I'm not using it much.'

Her remark came right out of the blue, as Marie-Claire's remarks so often seemed to. Joanne was a little embarrassed because she was already using the car. Had Marie-Claire noticed? She gave no sign that she had, so Joanne said nothing except, 'Thank you very much, Marie-Claire.' She caught an approving look from Daniel.

The Fiat was a snappy little vehicle and a joy to drive. Joanne felt very relaxed at the wheel and being independent made life much pleasanter. She could slip into Interlaken whenever she wanted to, and sometimes, if she got away from the clinic early enough, she would enjoy a stroll around the shops.

Esther commented on the fact that she was now mobile and Joanne told her that the car was Marie-Claire's, but she told no one else. Gerda, however, was also quick to notice.

'I see you've got yourself a car,' she commented one lunchtime.

'Yes, it makes life much easier not having to depend on other people for lifts,' said Joanne.

Gerda said enviously, 'I wish I could afford to buy a car.'

Esther, who was there at the time, said rather sharply, 'You could if you learned how to save money instead of wasting it on clothes you get sick of in a week!' Her irritation was showing because Gerda had apparently upset one of the patients unnecessarily.

Later a tight-lipped Esther said to Joanne, 'I've warned her a couple of times about her lackadaisical attitude. I don't want to speak to Luise about her, but I might have to.'

As the days went by, Joanne settled down very happily at the Harder-Kulm Clinic. She no longer felt overawed by the more famous or wealthy clients, and found many of them very interesting and often happy to talk to a nurse who was genuinely fascinated by their stories.

Sometimes she felt a pang of wistful regret for her old stamping ground at the Barmouth, but she knew she had done the right thing in cutting herself off from familiar places for the time being at least. She had hardly even thought of Luke since she'd been in Switzerland, and when she did think of him it was only to wonder if she had ever really been in love with him at all.

Although it snowed a lot and the ski-runs were in top condition everywhere, Joanne was not able to go skiing quite as soon as she had hoped. Bernard was unable to organise a day off to coincide with hers. Since she did not want to go alone, Joanne spent the day writing letters and postcards home. She half hoped to see something of Marie-Claire, who knew she was at home, but to her disappointment the girl did not stir from her room all day. Joanne was determined not to force herself on Marie-Claire, so she did not disturb her.

Before her next day off, Bernard announced triumphantly that he would be able to get the same day off. Joanne crossed her fingers and hoped nothing urgent would crop up to prevent it. Nothing did.

They drove to Lauterbrunnen and then travelled by funicular up to Mürren, along with a cheerful crowd of fellow-skiers. It was a crisply cold day, but the sky was clear and the sun shone. The mountain peaks stood out against the blue sky like cardboard scenery, painted for a stage show, the sharp contrasts of light and shadow emphasising their ruggedness. The lower slopes were a patchwork of green and white, and against the backdrop of magic mountain scenery, the picturesque Swiss chalets gave it all a picture-postcard charm.

'We have to take the cable-car next,' said Bernard, as they walked through the village of Mürren which nestled on a plateau high above the valley. On the other side rose the jagged peaks of the Eiger, the Jungfrau and the Mönch, prominent landmarks in the breathtaking panorama of the Alps.

'The longest cableway in the Alps,' Bernard told Joanne as the car slowly climbed the wire to the top of the Schilthorn. 'And the top is the starting point for the Inferno, the world's longest downhill race, which ends in Lauterbrunnen.'

'I'm sure it must be exhilarating,' said Joanne, 'but I'd never attempt it. I'm far from being an expert.'

They alighted from the cable-car at the summit of the Schilthorn, and she gasped at the view.

'This is like being on top of the world! It's fantastic!'

Bernard laughed. 'We Swiss become a little blasé about our mountains, but you are right, it is splendid.'

Joanne had hired skis for this trip and they were not a perfect fit, so she was not able to ski as comfortably as she might have done.

'Where's the best place to buy skis and boots?' she asked Bernard when they were having lunch in the revolving restaurant after several energetic runs.

She was thinking of Interlaken, but Beranard said, 'I have a friend in Berne who will fix you up better than anyone. We'll go there on your next day off.'

'That's very kind. . .'

He covered her hand with his. 'A pleasure, *meine Fräulein*!'

But in the end they did not go to Berne together on Joanne's next free day. Bernard was not able to get away because there was to be an urgent admission to the clinic that morning and he was needed there.

Joanne said, 'Never mind. I'll go anyway and do some other shopping, but I won't buy any skis until you can advise me. I need some clothes and I'll enjoy window-shopping. It would probably bore you to tears!'

His glance was admiring as well as teasing. 'You, Joanne, would never bore a man to tears!'

She laughed. 'Keep flattering me, Bernard. I can take lots of that!'

He slipped his arm around her shoulders and kissed her cheek, which startled her, because he had not been so familiar before. She was even more embarrassed when Daniel chose that moment to walk in. He raked them with a scathing look but did not comment.

Joanne did not see Daniel again that day and that evening, according to Luise, he dined at the home of his friend Elise Hoffmann, whom Marie-Claire had mentioned earlier.

'He's very fond of Elise,' Luise confided. 'There's some possibility they might marry.' She paused and made a rather doubtful face. 'They'll have to reach a compromise over their careers if they marry. They're both self-willed and ambitious, if in somewhat different ways. I'm fond of

Elise, but I fear their temperaments are likely to clash.'

'Happy marriages often have an element of conflict in them,' Joanne pointed out. 'It prevents life from becoming dull!'

Luise smiled. 'You're right, of course, but. . .' She shrugged. 'Young people must make their own decisions.'

Joanne was burning to ask her about Daniel's wife at that point, but she felt that might be too intrusive, and in any case, Elke brought their coffee and Luise changed the subject. Once again Marie-Claire had not appeared at dinner, and as Luise had some work to do, Joanne went up to her room early.

She was idly recalling her conversation with Luise about Daniel the previous night when next morning she was about to back the Fiat out of the garage to drive to Interlaken. She had decided to avoid driving around a strange city where there might be parking problems, by catching the train to the Swiss capital instead.

She jumped when Daniel suddenly appeared and bent to talk to her through the driving window.

'You're still going to Berne today?' he enquired. Evidently he knew that Bernard was not.

'Yes, but I'm going by train.'

He said, 'Since I'm going to Berne myself this morning, you might as well come with me. You can return by train. Why didn't you ask?'

Daniel went to Berne three days a week and usually stayed over Wednesday and Thursday nights. He had a small apartment in the city, Luise told Joanne. It simply had not occurred to Joanne to ask him for a lift. She was not certain now that she relished driving to Berne with him. He had a very disquieting effect on her whenever she was alone with him.

Her hesitation made him say, 'You wouldn't deprive me of the pleasure of your company for an hour or so, would you?' Faint mockery glimmered in the grey-blue eyes. 'Or perhaps you don't find the prospect of driving with me as attractive as with Dr Schmid?' He knew he sounded churlish and he wasn't quite sure why. Joanne was aggravating in a way he couldn't quite define, and yet there was something appealingly elusive about her that fascinated him. Quite apart from her sparkling green eyes. Her natural reserve often seemed like aloofness and yet her mouth quirked sometimes as though she was amused at private thoughts. At his expense!

Joanne's lips were quirking now, but only because she was telling herself not to be a fool. He couldn't eat her! Since she was not prepared to be rude in order to avoid going with him, she said a trifle impatiently, 'Not at all! I'm sure you're just as good a driver as Bernard!'

She swung her boots-clad legs out of the Fiat and felt his hand lightly on her arm as she stood up. The passenger door of the Mercedes was open, so she slid in obediently. She would have to get a taxi home from Interlaken, but she did not dare to bring that up as an excuse. He tucked the skirt of her dark green suit in and closed the door.

'It's a beautiful day,' she remarked as the car purred powerfully along the road. The lake was shimmering in the early morning sunlight and the mountains were clear of cloud.

'It is now,' Daniel murmured with a sideways glance at her and a friendly smile.

'Flattery will get you nowhere!' she retorted brightly, wishing her heart would stop its nervous fluttering. What was the matter with her today?

'Won't it? Not even if I keep it up? I gathered that you enjoyed flattery!'

His tongue was very firmly in his cheek and Joanne realised he must have overheard her lighthearted exchange with Bernard the day before. He glanced at her again and they both laughed. From then on Joanne felt more relaxed.

For the first few minutes, however, Daniel said little, and Joanne's attention was entirely absorbed by the picturesque scenery flashing past the window.

Eventually Daniel said, 'What made you take up psychiatric nursing?'

Joanne answered truthfully, 'I did my general training first, but after three years on the wards in the same hospital, I wanted a change. Naturally I often saw patients who needed to be referred to psychiatrists and I've always been interested in the connection between some physical and mental illnesses, and also in the public attitude to mental illness, the difficulties relatives have and . . .' She stopped, afraid she had said too much and was boring him.

But Daniel said, 'Go on. You were saying about attitudes.'

Joanne couldn't resist putting her point of view. 'It bothers me that for many people mental illness is still so—so taboo. It's as though having a disease of the mind isn't quite respectable, as though it's something not to mention, or something to be frightened of in the way physical diseases are not. It's no wonder it's difficult for some patients to get better!' She lowered her voice. 'You shouldn't have started me off!'

'Why not? I happen to agree with what you say. Mental illness is, however, often much more difficult for patients and families to cope with than physical illness. Sometimes it may not even seem like a real illness, or the manifestations can be difficult to come to terms with.'

'Yes, I know,' Joanne agreed, 'but no one should feel ashamed of having a mental illness, and relatives shouldn't think they need to hide the fact. It all helps to encourage misunderstandings and wrong generalisations. I think we ought to do more to explode some of the myths and educate the public into what mental illness is all about. Even in hospitals the attitudes are sometimes so—so Victorian!'

'Not at the Lord Barmouth, though,' he suggested, evidently acquainted with that institution.

'Oh, no, we're very progressive and enlightened there. We have a big programme aimed at helping patients to live in the community, and it's very successful. We're gradually breaking down the stigma of mental illness for many of our patients.'

He smiled. 'You talk as though you haven't quite cut your ties with the Barmouth!'

Joanne flushed. 'I keep forgetting I'm not there any more.'

She was surprised at Daniel's willingness to talk to her like this. He had seemed so aloof, yet this morning he had thawed and become more human. Usually, despite his unfailing politeness, she still felt intimidated and uneasily conscious of the fact that he had not wanted her to be employed in the first place. He would rather she'd stayed at the Lord Barmouth! Certainly, to date, she could report no progress with Marie-Claire that would justify her presence in the house. She ventured a few questions about his own career, but he was not very forthcoming. He seemed keener to continue the previous discussion.

Presently he said, 'You would have had a very wide-ranging experience at the Lord Barmouth, of course.'

'Yes, I certainly did. As you might imagine, I nursed a rather more mixed bag of patients than at the Harder-Kulm. Most of them were just ordinary people, of course. We never—or rarely—saw the wealthy or the famous who can afford the privacy provided by private clinics. We had none of the luxurious facilities you have either. Poor old Barmouth is always racking its brains for fund-raising ideas to raise a bit of extra cash.'

She caught a sidelong glance and was dismayed by the hardness in it. And his mouth had tightened perceptibly. What had she said?

He answered grittily, 'Whether patients are wealthy or famous or not is hardly relevant. They're all human beings in need of medical care. Exposure in a public hospital is undesirable for some people. They are sometimes more vulnerable than so-called ordinary people. And in fact, if you care to do a head count, you'll find that the Harder-Kulm cares for quite a number of ordinary people, as you call them.'

It was a strong double-edged rebuke and Joanne flinched under his castigating tone. 'I didn't mean to imply . . .' she began in mortification.

But he cut across her words. 'The Harder-Kulm and many other clinics like it exist because there's a need for them. If people wish to have a certain standard of luxury in their health care, then surely they have that right?'

Joanne made a valiant effort to rescue the situation. 'Of course, Daniel. I wasn't suggesting otherwise, any more than I was suggesting you and your mother don't have a right to run a clinic for profit.'

She could have bitten her tongue out for making the second quite unnecessary apology and badly phrasing it. The perceptible stiffening of his shoulders showed he did not even see it as such, and his features hardened even more with annoyance.

'I see, so you think the Harder-Kulm is simply a convenient money-spinner for my mother and me, pandering to the whims of the rich and famous instead of providing genuine health care? Perhaps to you it's not a bona fide medical institution.'

'Daniel! I didn't say that! You go too far. I think it's a very fine clinic.'

His glance was withering. He wasn't going to let her

redeem herself so easily. 'I'm surprised, Joanne, that regarding private clinics in the cynical way you seem to, you accepted a job in one. Do you deny that the prospect of meeting well-known people and nursing in comparative luxury didn't have a certain appeal for you?'

It was a cruel cut and Joanne had no ready answer. It would have sounded ridiculous to say she'd certainly had misgivings about the job. He wouldn't believe her. She had no intention either of revealing that she had decided to work abroad so as not to intrude on her father's new life, and she certainly wasn't going to admit that yes, the nature of the job had attracted her despite herself. She slumped back in her seat, humbled and unable to find anything to say.

Unaware she was doing it, she twisted her hands together in her lap, angry with herself for the stupid way she had spoiled everything. They'd been getting along so well, so perfectly in agreement, and she'd had to go and spoil it all with an ill-considered remark.

After a moment or two, Daniel took one hand off the wheel and reached across to cover hers and still their agitation.

'Sorry,' he murmured, 'I was a bit hard on you.'

Astonished, Joanne dared to glance at him. His brief glance at her still showed an unyielding expression in his eyes, but his mouth was twitching slightly at the corners as though in the beginnings of a smile.

'I think I deserved it,' she muttered contritely.

Daniel squeezed her hands briefly. 'You're entitled to your opinions, I'm afraid I overreacted.'

Joanne still felt all tied up in knots inside. She would almost have rather he hadn't apologised; somehow it made her feel worse. They were approaching the inner city now and in a few minutes they would part and go their separate ways. There was so much she wanted to say to make it right, properly right, between them, but she couldn't muster the right words. She was too afraid now of making a worse blunder. It irked greatly that once again she had shown herself in a less favourable light than she had intended.

A few minutes later, standing with her near the railway station, Daniel reeled off directions about where to go to shop and which sights she should see if she had time. When she protested that she would never remember it all, he responded by grabbing her arm and hurrying her into the station concourse, where he obtained a map and guidebook from the tourist information office there.

'You've no excuse for getting lost now,' he said.

'Thank you.' Joanne was overwhelmed by his thoughtfulness, especially as he must be, despite his apology, very displeased with her. If he'd dumped her and gone off in a huff, it would have been no more than she deserved.

He glanced at his watch. 'I must leave you now, I'm afraid. But if you need me for any reason, this is where my consulting rooms are.' He handed her a card, saying, 'You'll find the street marked on your map.'

It was almost an olive branch, Joanne thought, but the more civilly he behaved, the worse it made her feel.

'Don't spend all your francs!' he cautioned. *'Auf Wiedersehen!'*

'Auf Wiedersehen!' she whispered, but he had already gone.

For some time she wandered in a kind of daze, still thinking of the conversation in the car and castigating herself for her stupidity and rash tongue.

However, the shops soon exercised their fascination, and Joanne found herself tempted in all directions. She bought a few much-needed items like sweaters and splashed out on a couple of new dresses. Although she browsed around looking at skis and boots, she stuck to her decision to postpone their purchase until Bernard could accompany her.

For lunch she had coffee and *Apfelstrudel* in a cosy cafe while she studied the town guide Daniel had obtained for her. She was rather too laden with parcels to go sightseeing, and although the thought occurred that she could leave her parcels at his rooms she decided not to take advantage of his offer. She was still feeling too chastened to risk the possibility of confronting him again just yet.

She arrived back at the railway station just in time to catch a train and was struggling into a carriage when a hand reached out to help her. A man hoisted her carrier bags into the carriage and deposited them in the rack above an empty seat.

'*Dankeschön,*' Joanne said gratefully.

'You have been shopping, *Fräulein!*' he teased in English, evidently certain he had made the correct deduction about her.

'Yes. I think I may have overdone it a bit!' she said, sinking breathlessly into the seat just as the train began to move. He sat beside her.

'You are on holiday in Schweiz?'

'No, I'm working here. I'm a nurse.'

'Really? And where are you nursing?'

'At a clinic near Interlaken.'

His interest was immediate. 'You must have many rich and famous clients, *ja?*'

Joane shrugged, reminding herself to be cautious. She asked, 'Are you on holiday?'

'*Nein!* I am working too. I am a journalist.'

Joanne was glad she hadn't mentioned the name of the clinic, and to stop him being too curious she quickly asked a lot of questions about his work. He kept trying to probe about her work, however, and she wished she had not told him she was a nurse. She was very glad when he got off the train at Thun.

'I used to live in Interlaken,' he said, as he was leaving her. 'I visit my family there quite often. Perhaps we will meet some time.'

'Perhaps,' she said noncommittally, relieved that despite his flirtatious manner he had not suggested a definite meeting. Her coolness had evidently put him off.

When the train moved out of the station, she slumped back in her seat and let her mind drift back once more to the drive to Berne with Daniel. She would not see him again now until Friday evening, and suddenly that was cause for regret in spite of knowing that she had angered him.

It was nearly dark when Joanne lifted her bags down from the rack and prepared to alight at Interlaken West. She wouldn't make the same mistake as last time, she thought, with a grimace, and go to Ost!

When she arrived home, she went straight upstairs with her purchases, kicked off her shoes and made a cup of tea. On impulse she tapped on Marie-Claire's door and called out, 'Would you like to see what I bought today, Marie-Claire? You can tell me if I've wasted my money!'

She was pleased when, a few moments later, as she was laying her purchases out on the bed, Marie-Claire came in. Her manner was diffident, but she accepted a cup of tea and showed at least superficial interest in the clothes Joanne had bought. Joanne had not hoped for enthusiasm. Just the fact that she had come in was enough.

Marie-Claire also came down for dinner that evening, but she disappeared again immediately afterwards, and she said practically nothing during the meal.

Alone in the drawing room after dinner, Luise and Joanne discussed the new patient who had been admitted that day.

'A case of chronic schizophrenia,' said Luise. 'A young

man of only eighteen.' She looked questioningly at Joanne. 'By the way, have you read Daniel's book on schizophrenia?'

'No, I don't think I have,' Joanne replied.

'It's a very good clinical study, but of course he was also able to write from personal experience.' When Joanne looked startled, Luise continued, 'No, not himself—his wife. He hasn't told you about Ingrid? No, he probably wouldn't. He rarely speaks about her now.' She stirred her coffee reflectively. 'It all happened some years ago. Ingrid and Daniel were married very young. He was still at medical school and she was studying music. She was diagnosed as having chronic schizophrenia when she was about twenty-two. It was a very gradual onset as it so often is, and there must have been signs that passed unrecognised for years. Daniel qualified as a general practitioner but studied psychiatry later, because of Ingrid.'

Now Joanne was beginning to understand Daniel's intense feelings about Marie-Claire. Before she could say that Marie-Claire had mentioned Daniel's wife, Luise sighed deeply and said, 'It was a very hard time for Daniel. She refused to be hospitalised, and one day she just walked out and disappeared. It was some days before she was found, and only then because her car was involved in an accident. Ingrid was killed. Daniel has always blamed himself because he feels he ought to have been able to prevent it.'

'How terrible!' Joanne said in a whisper.

'Yes, it was,' Luise went on. 'After her death, Daniel determined to devote himself to research into the condition, and he has written several papers as well as two books—the second is still in draft form. He has some interesting ideas. I'll ask him to let you read both of them— you may find them helpful.' Her suddenly unguarded look confirmed the suspicion in Joanne's mind.

'He's afraid that Marie-Claire is also schizophrenic, isn't he?' said Joanne. Schizophrenia was almost always a disease of the young, often brought on by drastic changes in the life of a patient. Diagnosis was often difficult as several other conditions could be confused with it, especially in the early stages.

Luise nodded and smiled a little shakily. 'We see disturbed people every day in our work, but it's still hard when illness is in one's own family.'

'Of course it is,' Joanne sympathised.

'What do you think?' asked Luise.

Joanne was surprised to be asked for her opinion. She answered cautiously, 'I can understand Daniel's concern, and also his reluctance to make a definite diagnosis. It doesn't really help much to put a label on something.'

Luise nodded and said softly, 'I know my perspective is somewhat subjective, since I'm her mother.'

Joanne now realised the special significance of some of Luise's questions at her interview in London regarding her expereince with patients suffering from schizophrenia.

Luise seemed to want to talk about her worries, and she went on, 'The trouble with Daniel is that he divides himself up into too many parts. I wish sometimes he would give up the Foundation and let the trustees run it, but I know he feels a duty towards it because it was his father's wish that he should carry on with it. But with his work here and his Berne practice and other consulting he does, he takes on too much.'

'Doctors usually do,' Joanne said resignedly, and asked, 'What is the Foundation?'

'Hasn't he mentioned that either?'

Joanne shook her head and did not remind Luise that she scarcely ever saw Daniel to talk to for more than a couple of minutes at a time, except in the house at dinner and afterwards. And he certainly hadn't told her much this morning.

Luise explained, 'It's the Eric Peterson Foundation. Have you not heard of it?'

Joanne was astonished. 'But of course I have! It provides care for handicapped children and their families in England, and especially the intellectually handicapped. It has connections with the Barmouth where I worked...' She broke off, realising that she could have bumped into Daniel there some time and never known it. Or could she? Somehow she felt sure she would have remembered those grey-blue eyes.

'It was founded by Sir Eric Peterson,' Luise said proudly. 'My husband, Daniel's father.'

'It never occurred to me to connect the name. Peterson is a common enough surname,' said Joanne. 'Even Daniel saying his father was English didn't prompt me. Of course I've read some of Eric Peterson's books on child psychology,' she added, and thought, why didn't he tell me about this?

'Eric handed over the chairmanship of the Foundation to Daniel just before he died,' Luise explained. 'Daniel trips back and forth to England frequently—too often, in my opinion. He should concentrate his energies in one place. But he doesn't take advice from me!' She shrugged helplessly. 'He also feels duty bound to assist me at the clinic because he knows Eric would have wanted him to. He refuses to take a penny out of it for himself, however. His fees are paid straight into the Foundation which, despite its strong financial position and good management, is always in need of more money to fund new research projects.'

While Daniel's mother was talking, Joanne felt a slow burning sensation creeping over her face and neck. And she had virtually accused Daniel of pandering to rich clients in order to make money! No wonder he had been angry! She felt quite sick. How was she going to face him now she knew the truth? She felt she could crawl out into the snow and die of shame.

Luise, seemingly unaware of her discomfort, talked on about the Foundation and its activities, but Joanne was finding it hard to concentrate. All she could see in her mind's eye was Daniel's angry expression.

CHAPTER FIVE

'How was Berne?' asked Esther with a knowing look when Joanne arrived for work next day. She was checking the drugs cupboard, and Joanne joined her to assist.

'I had a great day. I spent too much money, of course! Was it frantic here?'

'No, it was very quiet. Our new client settled down rather well and is being very co-operative. He seems to have taken an instant liking to Bernard, which is a most promising start.' Esther glanced slyly at Joanne. 'Bernard was a bit put out, I think, at your gallivanting off with Daniel.'

Joanne hadn't expected anyone to know that. 'Why should he be put out? He couldn't go himself.' She picked up a box of disposable syringes and held them poised for a moment before starting to count. 'He knows Daniel goes to Berne on Wednesdays. He should have guessed he'd give me a lift.'

Esther shrugged. 'He certainly looked a bit surprised when Gerda said she'd seen you driving through Interlaken with him.'

Joanne felt a bit nettled. 'Gerda likes making mischief if she can.'

Esther laughed. 'Don't take it to heart! Your private life is never your own in a small community. And here, because you're a foreigner, everyone is interested in you. You won't have as much privacy as at home. I'd better warn you that Gerda or Gerda's mother will have told everyone they know by now!'

Joanne sighed. 'It doesn't matter. I suppose it's well-known by now that I live in Luise's house, and no doubt that's given rise to speculation. Actually, there wasn't much privacy at the Barmouth. I'm used to gossip. Hospitals have a better information service than the BBC!'

Esther finished counting some capsules and ticked off the quantity on her list. 'I hope the pharmaceuticals supplier comes today. We're low on Mogadon and we need supplies of most of our neuroleptics.'

'Anything special you want me to do today?' asked Joanne, re-stacking the cupboard neatly.

Esther considered. 'Luise is rather worried about Elsa. She's still losing weight and we suspect she's tricking us despite all our precautions. She gets on well with you, so would you try and keep a closer eye on her for a few days?'

'You mean she's pretending to eat, but is hiding food and disposing of it later?'

'Possibly. It's incredible how cunning they can be! She may have a secret supply of laxatives, or she may be eating and then inducing vomiting afterwards. Bernard found her looking at some fashion magazines yesterday and just about every page had a broomstick model on it. I don't think that helps!'

'Her parents haven't been to see her recently, have they?'

'No, which Daniel thinks is a good thing, since they seem to upset her. They're not very sympathetic. They seem to think she ought to just pull herself together and stop being stupid. They keep on about how they've done everything for her and this is how she repays them.'

'Unfortunately a rather typical attitude,' remarked Joanne.

Esther nodded. 'We don't want to treat her like a prisoner, but we need to keep a stricter eye on her—find an excuse to be around when she has her midday meal and afterwards for a while. That might help.' She ticked off the last item on her list. 'Good, that's finished. Would you get Ilse to type up the list of what we need, and when she's done that, would you mind getting Bernard to authorise it?'

Joanne took Esther's list to the secretary and presently collected the typed forms and finally ran Bernard to earth to check it with her and authorise it.

He said, 'Come along to my office.' Joanne knew he would ask her about Daniel. 'Did you enjoy your day in Berne?' he asked, his eyes raking her face searchingly. He seemed a little cool.

'Very much,' she said. 'Daniel gave me a lift as he was going anyway. I got a street map from the tourist information office at the railway station, and I had no trouble finding my way around. I loaded myself up with too much shopping to go sightseeing, but I looked around at skis and boots quite thoroughly. I think I know what I want, but I left buying them until you can go with me.'

He looked somewhat mollified by this. 'Which I hope will be soon,' he said, smiling at her.

Joanne took the drugs list back to Esther and then checked on who had appointments with the hairdresser and manicurist, both of whom would be visiting the clinic that day.

Some of the patients ate their meals in a communal dining room, but some had meals served in their rooms or suites. Elsa ate privately, which made strict supervision, if it were not to be obtrusive, rather a problem.

Near lunchtime, Joanne found an excuse to visit the girl

and she remained chatting until the midday meal was served.

'Mmm, that smells delicious,' she remarked as the maid set the plates on the table. 'I hope we're having the same!'

Elsa wrinkled her nose. 'Ugh, it smells horrible!'

'Would you rather have something else?' Joanne offered at once. 'What do you fancy?'

Elsa gave her a withering glance. 'Nothing. All the food here is awful. They only give me food to make me fat.'

'It might if you ate enough of it,' said Joanne lightly, 'but the amount you put away wouldn't fatten a fly!'

'Let the flies have it!' said Elsa with a grim smile.

Joanne spotted the magazines Esther had mentioned scattered about and idly picked one up and turned the pages. A sudden thought occurred to her. 'Would you like to be a model, Elsa?' she asked casually.

A glitter came into the girl's usually dull eyes. 'Oh, yes!' She sagged. 'No. My parents wouldn't allow it. They despise that kind of career. They wish me to be a pianist like Maria, my sister, or a singer like Mama.' She shrugged. 'But I have no talent for anything.'

Joanne looked her over. 'I think you'd make a marvellous model. But you know, even compared to the women in these pictures, you're too skinny. Your bones are just a bit too prominent, and there's a point, you know, when salt-cellars start to look like malnutrition.'

Elsa eyed her cagily.

Joanne went on, 'If you were to put on a few pounds it would make all the difference. You need to soften those curves just a little bit. And besides, a model needs a great deal of stamina, and you need to eat well for that. It would be no good feeling tired all the time.'

Elsa's mouth was a stubborn line. She did not answer, but Joanne suspected there was a certain amount of conflict going on inside her over what Joanne had said.

Then all at once a wild idea occurred to Joanne and she said impulsively, 'I know someone who could advise you. She might even be able to help you get started on a modelling career. Would you like to talk to her?'

Elsa showed a faint spark of interest. 'But my parents...' she said dismally, hopelessness in her large vivacious brown eyes. 'They would never approve.'

Joanne said boldly, 'I think they might, Elsa, if it was properly explained to them. You leave that to me. I'll try to work something out, I promise, but meanwhile, how about seeing if the food really is as bad as you think? Let's say you aim at putting on three kilos. That's about what you need, I think, but we'll ask Marianne.' She surveyed Elsa's wraith-like figure as she spoke, knowing it would need rather more than three kilos, but to mention too much at first would only make the girl rebel. No wonder Luise was worried about her! The girl was going to collapse again if they weren't careful. She would simply starve to death.

Elsa looked doubtful, but she sat down at the table. She grimaced at first, but finally she ate the food slowly and laboriously while Joanne chatted and thumbed through the magazines, making comments on the fashions.

At last Elsa pushed the plate aside. 'It wasn't bad,' she conceded.

Joanne smiled. 'It makes me drool just watching you! Now, promise me you'll try and put on those few kilos in the next couple of weeks. If you promise to do that I'll ask Marianne to come and talk to you.'

'Who's she?'

Joanne said airily 'Oh, I think you'll recognise her!' Marianne's picture was in several of the magazines.

'Is she a client here?'

Joanne nodded. 'Now, no more questions. Are you going to promise?'

Elsa heaved a sigh, gave Joanne a faint smile and

nodded. 'All right'.

Joanne went to lunch wondering how she could possibly have been so rash as to make promises to Elsa she didn't know she could keep. What if Marianne wouldn't help? Or Luise might be outraged and forbid her to ask the French model to help Elsa. In the end she confided first in Esther, who was mildly shocked but sympathetic.

'Perhaps you were a bit hasty,' she said, but with an understanding smile, 'but at least you seem to have aroused her interest. It's the parents that will be the problem.'

'That will be up to Daniel,' said Joanne firmly. 'Elsa is his patient, isn't she? He'll have to give her parents some very serious counselling.'

Esther pursed her lips. 'Well, I'll leave it up to you to break the news to him!'

'Do I need his permission or Luise's to talk to Marianne?' asked Joanne. 'I'm sure she'd be willing to help Elsa. And I'm sure the girl does have potential as a model.'

'I suggest you talk it over with Luise,' Esther advised.

On Friday afternoon Daniel telephoned the clinic and said he'd had trouble with his car and would have to leave it in Berne for servicing. He asked Ilse to ask Joanne if she would mind meeting his train.

Joanne had no option but to do so, although the thought of it made her insides flutter. The drive to Berne on Wednesday was vividly in her mind still, and her trepidation was increased now because of Elsa. Luise had been cautious but, to Joanne's relief, co-operative about the plan, and to Joanne's even greater relief, Marianne had happily agreed to talk to the girl.

They had not met before and at their first meeting that morning had seemed to get along very well. Joanne felt more than a little gratified when Luise said she thought it might do Marianne good too. A protégé might be just the diversion she needed.

Daniel, of course, did not know about it yet, and as Elsa was his patient after all, and it was Daniel who would have to agree to talk to her parents, he might well accuse Joanne of interference. Even Luise's support might not stop him being angry.

Joanne went to meet the train wondering if she should mention Elsa right away or not. If she didn't he might later believe it was because she expected him to be angry. But every time she rehearsed the words she got the jitters, and in the end she decided she would only be defensive, so it was better to let Luise tell him.

'Coward!' she said to herself as she saw the train approaching. Her heart was fluttering unnaturally because she dreaded seeing Daniel again yet felt strangely excited by the prospect.

She saw him at a distance, striding towards the car, carrying a large briefcase and with his coat collar turned up because it was starting to snow. Her heart suddenly leapt with pleasure instead of dread.

His expression was stern, just as it had been when she had insulted him on the way to Berne, but as he flung himself into the Fiat beside her and turned to her, it broke into a smile. Joanne felt as though her bones had melted away, leaving only the marrow behind. She felt almost too weak to put the car into gear.

He removed his gloves and clasped her hand. '*Guten Tag*, Joanne.'

'Hello, Daniel.'

His large hand remained closed around hers for a moment and she felt embarrassed as she eventually withdrew her hand, as though she had clung to his on purpose.

On the way home he enquired if she had had a successful

day in Berne, and she tried not to prattle about it, although she was anxious to fill in the mercifully short time with remarks that did not involve the clinic.

Daniel was his usual pleasant polite self, but there was a constraint between them nonetheless, Joanne felt. The shadow of her insult and his anger still hovered between them. She was glad when they reached the house and the moment she had dreaded, that he might just happen to mention Elsa, thus obliging her to confess what she had done, was no longer a danger.

Instead, as they went inside, he asked, 'How are you getting along with Marie-Claire?'

'She showed some interest in my shopping trip and last night we had quite a long chat before bed. I'm trying to make a habit of our nightly chats, so it seems quite natural, not some sort of imposed therapy.'

'Very good.' He lowered his voice as they entered the hall. 'My mother told me on the phone the other night that you would be particularly interested to read what I've written on schizophrenia, especially as we have a new client at the clinic with the condition.'

'Yes, I would like to,' Joanne told him. 'Your mother told me you're writing another book on the subject.' If Luise had mentioned Elsa to him, he was not letting on. Saving his reprimand for a later more private interview, perhaps, she though nervously.

He said, 'Yes, it's a kind of handbook for families of sufferers of the disease. I hope other people will read it too. There's so much misunderstanding, I've tried to explode some of the myths.'

Joanne felt a little hurt that he had not told her about it when they had been discussing attitudes to mental disease, but perhaps he preferred not to talk about work in progress. She said, 'It sounds like a book that's greatly needed. I get so mad when I hear people who know nothing about it confusing it with split personality, which is totally different and very rare.'

He was smiling at her enthusiasm. 'And classically illustrated in films like *The Three Faces of Eve*,' he said, adding, 'I've tried to explain in lay terms exactly what a split mind is and how it differs from split personality. You must tell me if I haven't made myself absolutely clear.'

'You don't have to let me read the new manuscript,' Joanne assured him, feeling he was probably wishing his mother hadn't mentioned it to her.

'I know,' he said, 'but your comments may be useful.'

Their eyes met and his were unfathomable. Joanne was sure her nervousness must show and that he must wonder what she was so edgy about. All he said, however, was, 'I shall be working in my study after dinner tonight. Come in and I'll look out some other literature for you as well as my own.'

While she was changing for dinner, Joanne made up her mind. She would apologise properly to him for her rudeness on Wednesday. She would tell him that Luise had told her about the Foundation. That was, she thought wryly, if he hadn't already hauled her over the coals for taking the law into her own hands over Elsa.

To give herself moral support, she wore one of the new dresses she had bought in Berne, a finely pleated crêpe in soft silvery grey with white edgings on the mandarin collar and wrists.

She came out of her room at the same time as Marie-Claire, who had evidently decided to join them for dinner. Joanne was surprised to see the girl wearing a dress, and she had coiled her hair up and fastened it in a sophisticated style with combs. It was the first time Joanne had seen Marie-Claire in a dress.

'Hello, you look very glamorous!' Joanne greeted her, eyeing the elegant purple wool shantung rather enviously.

It was clearly a couturier model and its soft draping moulded Marie-Claire's figure attractively. Its simple lines were set off by a single strand of pearls and pearl earrings. Marie-Claire was also wearing a touch of lipstick for the first time.

Her expression, however, was as blank as usual, even though she smiled faintly. 'Thank you. I haven't worn this dress for a long time. It was part of my trousseau.' Joanne caught her breath. Marie-Claire had never made any reference to her marriage, even obliquely, before. Now she added, 'Your dress is very pretty, Joanne. That's one you bought in Berne, isn't it?'

Joanne was pleased that she had noticed. 'Yes, I bought more than I should have, but there were so many lovely things. One shop assistant asked me if I was buying a trousseau!'

Marie-Claire was surprised. 'Are you getting married?'

'No! Of course not.' Joanne decided to change the subject quickly in case talking about weddings proved to be unwise. They went downstairs talking about skiing.

Daniel was just going into the drawing room. He placed a hand on each girl's shoulder. 'What a peach of a pair! How charming you both look!'

Joanne flushed, but Marie-Claire walked on into the room without making any response at all. Catching Daniel's eye, Joanne saw how pleased and surprised he was to see Marie-Claire coming to dinner in a dress, nevertheless.

If it was progress, it was only a small step. Marie-Claire, as usual, said very little, either while they were having an aperitif or at dinner, and straight afterwards she drifted back to her room, asking Elke to bring her coffee there. Luise had to go out almost immediately after dinner, and Joanne, remembering that Daniel had said he had work to do, said as soon as they were alone, 'If you'd like to give me

that reading material you promised now, I could browse
through it before I go to bed.'

He refilled his coffee cup and hers. 'Bring your coffee
into my study.'

It was the first time Joanne had entered his study. It was a
more sombre room than Luise's den, wood-panelled and
with one wall book-lined. Besides the desk there were
armchairs, a couch and a coffee table. The windows were
heavily draped in dark blue velvet.

'Sit down, Joanne,' Daniel invited, and she chose an
armchair reluctantly because she had no intention of
staying long. She was uncomfortably aware that the Elsa
business had still not been mentioned. Luise would have
avoided doing so at dinner, of course, because of Marie-
Claire's presence. But for the moment there was
something more important on her mind which she was
trying to gather the courage to say.

Daniel opened a filing cabinet and while his broad back
was turned to her, Joanne framed her apology and blurted
it out.

'Daniel—I want to apologise. . .'

Before she could get any further, he had swung round.
'Apologise? What have you done?'

It wasn't easy now he was facing her. Joanne gulped and
tried not to meet his gaze, but his eyes compelled her. 'For
all the crass things I said on Wednesday—or implied—I
had no idea you were connected with the Eric Peterson
Foundation. I really did weigh in there. . .'

He strode across the room. 'Who told you about the
Foundation?'

'Your mother. It happened to come up in conversation
the other night. I—I just wanted you to know that I'm a
great admirer of the Foundation's work, but it never
occurred to me to connect it with you, and as you hadn't
mentioned it. . .' She broke off. There was no need to make

excuses for herself. 'I—I feel very ashamed and a bit of a fool.'

'There's no need to put on sackcloth *and* ashes!' he said dryly, and then with a smile gathering at the corners of his mouth, 'My dear Joanne, it doesn't matter in the least to me that you formed some very natural misconceptions about the Harder-Kulm, my mother and me.'

But it had at the time, she thought. There was no getting away from that, whatever he said.

He went on, 'I'm not blaming you for disapproving. . .'

'Daniel, I don't disapprove!' she denied desperately. 'It's just. . .'

'It's not really your cup of tea, is it? You don't feel entirely comfortable in surroundings like the Harder-Kulm, do you?'

Joanne took a deep breath. She might as well be honest. Daniel was too perceptive to lie to. 'I like working there, Daniel, and I do think it's an excellent clinic in every way, but yes, I suppose you're right, and deep down it isn't quite what I'm cut out for.'

And now he would tell her to pack her bags and go back to the Barmouth, she thought, and wondered why the prospect of doing that suddenly hurt so much.

'At least you're honest!' he said rather wryly. 'Perhaps it will make you feel better if I tell you that most of the income from the clinic goes to the Foundation.'

'Your mother told me you don't take a penny. . .'

He went on as though she hadn't spoken, 'My mother has an income, of course, but neither I nor Marie-Claire take a franc. By the terms of our father's will only the Foundation benefits. Marie-Claire has her own money— not great wealth, I assure you, since Paolo Valli was not a thrifty young man!'

'You make me feel worse,' wailed Joanne.

Daniel bent down and placed his hands on the arms of

the chair and his face was very close to hers. 'We wouldn't dream of forcing you to honour your contract if you weren't happy here, but my mother and I both hope you'll stay with us for the duration of it. You've fitted in very well. We wouldn't like to lose you, either from the hospital or from here.'

Nothing could have gratified Joanne more than to hear him say he accepted her, not just as a nurse at the clinic but as being of some use to Marie-Claire.

He went on, 'I don't want to hear any more apologies. Rather, I should be the one begging your pardon for being so touchy and resenting criticism that wasn't intended. Shall we agree to forget it?'

'Yes—all right,' murmured Joanne. But there was still the business about Elsa, she thought. He might change completely towards her when he heard about that. She wished in a way she could summon the courage to tell him now, but she just couldn't.

'And now. . .' He crossed back to the filing cabinet and withdrew a folder of clippings from medical journals. Then he took a couple of books from the shelves. 'This will be enough for you to be going on with.' He placed the folder and books on one arm of her chair and sat in the adjoining chair, reaching across to the table for his coffee.

For a few moments he seemed absorbed in private thoughts, then he surprised Joanne by saying, 'Did my mother also tell you why I have a special interest in schizophrenia?'

'Yes, she did,' Joanne said softly. 'I hope you don't mind.' She added quickly, 'There's no need to talk about it. It must still be very painful for you.'

Daniel rested his elbows on the chair arms and steepled his fingers, resting his chin on them. 'For a while it was—very painful,' he said slowly, 'but I think I've got over it now. One must be positive. I did think of writing a personal experience kind of book, but that seemed too much of a self-indulgence, or. . .' he smiled faintly, '. . .or a therapy. Besides, my story didn't have a happy ending, and since all stories don't end that way, my aim is to give encouragement. There's a great deal of hope for sufferers of schizophrenia even in its worst forms. Those who can't be cured can usually have their symptoms alleviated.'

Joanne was touched that he was talking to her in such a deeply personal way. She asked, 'When will your new book be published?' She had noticed that the manuscript was not amongst the material he had given her, so perhaps he'd had second thoughts about allowing her to read it after all.

He pulled a rather wry face. 'When I can find someone to type it for me! I'm not anxious to send it to an agency, and the woman who used to do my private typing and who was one hundred per cent discreet has left the practice and the region. I don't feel I can ask her successor to take on any extra work just yet, but it's becoming rather urgent to find someone who's willing to battle with my scrawl. My publisher is anxious to see the draft.'

Joanne did not hesitate. 'I can type, Daniel,' she said impulsively. 'I have very little to do in the evenings. If you can get me a typewriter I'd be happy to do it.' She paused, adding doubtfully, 'That is if you think. . .well, if you'd like me to do it.'

He looked startled. 'You? But it's a lot of work, and there'll need to be a lot of re-drafting.'

'I don't mind that.'

He stroked his chin. 'Are you sure your typing is up to such a big job?'

Joanne pretended to be affronted. 'I don't type with two fingers! I learned properly. I did a commercial course before I decided to become a nurse. I used to type my father's reports more often than not.'

'But you work all day,' he objected. 'It would be an

imposition.'

'You evidently didn't think it was on your former secretary,' she pointed out.

He chuckled. 'All right! And I'll pay you, of course.' He tapped the tips of his fingers together. 'I have to admit it would be wonderful to have the work done right here where I can answer your queries promptly. But perhaps you should give it some thought first. You might decide it would be too much to take on.'

Joanne was definite. 'I'm sure it isn't such an enormous book! If it is, it must need cutting or no one will read it. You're not writing a massive medical treatise on the subject, are you? Just a helpful, practical book for people who have to cope with schizophrenia. I'm sure I can cope,' she finished a trifle dryly.

Daniel stood up and Joanne rose too. She reached for their cups and saucers, intending to take them to the kitchen, but he said, 'Leave the cups. Elke will fetch them later.' His fingers brushed hers, and an alarming shock ran through her and stirred feelings deep inside her that seemed never to have been stirred before.

She picked up the folder and books he had lent her, tucking the folder under her arm, but she was so disconcerted by him, she managed to fumble with them and they all slid to the floor. Embarrassed, she bent to retrieve them, and Daniel also crouched down, so that some confusion ensued as they both clutched the same item. Straightening up, Joanne found herself grasping the file in one hand while the other hand was firmly enclosed in his. He held out the books to her.

'Sorry. . .' she murmured, flustered by his nearness, and almost dropping the books again as he thrust them into her hands.

Then, in a totally unexpected gesture, he ran the tips of his fingers lightly around the shape of her face, a strangely wistful kind of smile flitting across his mouth. His lips moved as though he was about to say something, but instead he bent his head and matched them to hers with gentle pressure.

The kiss was so fleeting that afterwards in her room, Joanne wondered if she had imagined it all. Yet surely no figment of the imagination could have left her feeling so lightheaded and trembling like a leaf. She barely remembered stumbling up the stairs clutching the reading material tightly to her chest in case she dropped it again, and long after the light was out that night, she was still staring into the darkness and feeling that light brushing of his flesh against hers.

Her encounter with Daniel was only slightly more startling, however, than that with Marie-Claire as she reached her room. Marie-Claire was waiting at the top of the stairs, and Joanne had the uncomfortable feeling that those glazed blue-grey eyes saw more than it appeared. She was sure the flush on her cheeks and her breathlessness must give her away.

Displaying the books, she said in as casual a tone as she could muster, 'Daniel has given me some homework!' She did not reveal yet that she was going to type his new manuscript. Marie-Claire was always so prickly about Daniel.

Marie-Claire did not comment. She merely said, 'Next time you and Bernard go skiing, I'll come.'

Joanne nearly fell over. Marie-Claire's remarks usually were those least expected, but this was a bombshell—a very heartening one.

'Will you? That's great. Bernard is going to help me buy some skis and boots next week and then we'll go skiing at the first opportunity we get after that. I suppose you've got all the gear you need, Marie-Claire, or would you like to come shopping with us?'

Marie-Claire ventured a smile but shook her head. 'I don't need to go shopping, thank you, Joanne.' She inclined her head thoughtfully. 'I used to ski with Bernard a long time ago...' And all at once the rigidity returned to her expression.

'Are we having hot *schokolade* tonight?' Joanne asked.

'I'll make it,' said Marie-Claire.

That was another promising step, Joanne thought. Usually she was the one to make the supper drink while Marie-Claire sat passively waiting.

They chatted in Marie-Claire's room for half an hour, but for once Joanne's mind was scarcely on what she was saying, it was downstairs in Daniel's study reliving that fleeting but unforgettable kiss.

CHAPTER SIX

THE NEXT morning Joanne wondered if Daniel would be going to the clinic today and would want a lift, since his car was in Berne being serviced. She saw nothing of him, however, and received no request, so when she noticed that Luise's car had already gone, she assumed he must have gone with his mother, or else was not seeing clients there today.

Joanne felt very uneasy about seeing him again, partly because of the Elsa business and partly now because of having been kissed by him. As she drove to the clinic the mountains seemed to look positively ominous that morning.

Esther was on duty, and her opening remarks did nothing to make Joanne feel optimistic.

'Daniel's in a strange mood,' she said. 'Was he all right last night or suffering withdrawal symptoms because of having no car?'

Joanne managed to laugh. 'I didn't notice anything strange. What do you mean?'

'Withdrawn—preoccupied. Almost as though he's annoyed with himself over something.'

For being too familiar with her? Joanne wondered. A ripple of indignation ran through her. Didn't he think she could take casual kisses as nonchalantly as anyone else? Surely he wasn't afraid she would try to make something of it?

When he sent for her during the morning, she reacted

first by trying wildly to think of an excuse for postponing the interview, because she knew it was bound to be about Elsa. Daniel had been with Elsa for some time, just prior to the summons. But there was no putting it off. She had to face up to it. With a wry little smile to herself, she suddenly remembered Marie-Claire saying, 'They won't bite you!' Why was she behaving like a coward?

When she knocked, he called, *'Herein!'*

'You wanted to see me?' Joanne entered only halfway.

'Come in, come in,' Daniel said impatiently. He rose and came to the front of the desk. He looked formidable, Joanne thought, or was it just her nerves? 'Sit down, Joanne.' He sounded stern.

She sat, trying to relax in the white vinyl armchair and not succeeding very well. She was too conscious of his grey-blue eyes assessing her, and she was remembering too vividly the feel of his lips on hers, his arms encircling her. He leaned against the desk and folded his arms across his chest. He was wearing a blue and white striped shirt, she noticed, fixing her gaze just below his chin, on a blue and black tie with a gold pin in it.

Daniel came straight to the point. 'So you had an idea how to encourage Elsa to eat?'

Joanne inadvertently looked up into his steely gaze. She tried not to show she was flustered. 'Well—er—yes. . .I—er—discussed it with Luise. . .' she faltered helplessly while he regarded her steadily.

'After you'd set the plan in motion, however,' he remarked dryly, while Joanne's cheeks flamed. 'A rather ambitious plan, isn't it?'

'Yes, I'm sorry. . .' She lowered her gaze slightly. 'I know I shouldn't have been so impetuous, but it just sort of—happened. I was talking to her and. . .'

'You trapped yourself into making promises you didn't know whether you would be able to fulfil,' he said sternly.

Joanne was too miserable to see the ghost of a twinkle in his eyes. 'I know. I should have thought it all out before I said anything and I should have spoken to you or Luise first before I tried to get Elsa interested, but I didn't because at the time I—I had to strike while the iron was hot, if you know what I mean.' She lifted her chin a little, feeling bolder all at once because telling him about it had suddenly made her feel justified. 'I believe we should sometimes act on our intuition. We're dealing with human beings, not machines!'

Now I've done it, she thought. I've spoken rashly again and he'll have every right to dismiss me. She concentrated her gaze on the Paul Klee painting just to the right of his face and on the wall behind him.

'Joanne, look at me!'

Reluctantly, she brought her gaze back to meet his once more. To her surprise it was not anger she saw but a widening smile. He shook his head slowly from side to side and lightly tapped the forefinger of one hand in the palm of the other.

'What's the matter? Were you expecting me to be angry with you for manipulating my clients without my permission? Is that why you didn't tell me last night about this?' He seemed to be more annoyed by the omission than anything else.

She nodded. 'I thought Luise would have told you—and there wasn't really an opportunity.'

'No,' he agreed, his eyes still steadily on her face. 'No, there wasn't, was there?'

'I know it was a bit unethical to involve Marianne,' Joanne admitted, 'but I was sure she would be willing to help Elsa, and she is. Have you talked to her too?' After all, she thought, the plan was working so far. Elsa was interested—and eating her food. And Marianne was quite enthusiastic about encouraging her.

Daniel said, 'Yes, I've talked to Marianne. I have to say that you've shown considerable sensitivity and ingenuity, and I only wish I'd thought of such a plan myself. I'm not unaware of the mutual benefit patients can sometimes obtain from each other. But I have to caution you not to allow your success on this occasion to tempt you to try and repeat it too often or when the circumstances are not so auspicious.'

'Oh, I'm not likely to do that,' Joanne assured him, relieved that he was not angry after all.

He was smiling again. 'I'm not against nurses having as free a hand as possible in the day-to-day treatment of clients. You get to know them better than anybody, and they often trust the nurses far more than their psychiatrists.' His expression suddenly became grave and he sighed. 'I wish a similar solution could be found for Marie-Claire.'

Joanne nodded, but was glad that today she could at least offer the positive encouragement of, 'I'm sure she's making progress, Daniel. She wants to go skiing with Bernard and me.' She had quite forgotten this startling news, with so many other things on her mind.

His eyebrows rose, and there was cautious hope in his eyes. 'She has said so?'

'Yes, last night. She said that next time Bernard and I go skiing she wants to come too. That's all right, isn't it?'

'Yes, of course, but. . .' Daniel frowned anxiously, 'you must be careful not to rush her.'

Joanne shook her head. 'Don't worry, I'll be very careful.' She understood that Daniel's anxiety was all the greater because Marie-Claire was his sister. And there was the spectre of Ingrid hanging over him. He was naturally afraid that Marie-Claire might come to harm, and if she did as a result of something he had condoned, he would again blame himself.

Joanne said, 'If she changes her mind, which is highly likely, I won't pressure her. We'll only do what comes naturally. I'll play it by ear.'

'Intuition,' he said with a smile, and with a curiously searching look. 'Is that how you believe life should be lived?'

'On intuition? Yes, I suppose so—well, most of the time. If I've got a gut feeling about something...' She pulled a wry face. 'Not very scientific, is it?'

'It's not possible to be wholly scientific about human nature,' he observed, and there seemed to be a wealth of meaning in the words that she had no access to.

There was a long pause while he looked steadily into her face. Joanne wanted to go, but couldn't quite bring herself to make a move. Fortunately, the door flew open and Luise came in.

'Oh, Daniel—I'm sorry, I didn't realise. . .' She smiled when she saw Joanne. 'I wouldn't interrupt, only. . .'

'I was just going,' said Joanne, and escaped without a backward glance at Daniel. Her heart was singing now because he hadn't really been angry after all. He'd been right to rebuke her, of course, so she didn't get over-confident about taking matters into her own hands, but at least he hadn't been unreasonable.

'What's the matter with you? Won a lottery?' It was Gerda confronting her in the corridor.

'Eh—what?' Joanne had been miles away.

'You were singing to yourself.'

'Was I?' Joanne's face broke into an amazed grin. 'No, I haven't won anything. At least, I suppose I might have done in a way.' At Gerda's puzzled expression, she added, 'Don't worry, I was just feeling happy, that's all.'

'Nice for you to have a reason,' said Gerda moodily, and swept on.

When Joanne and Bernard arranged to go to Berne for the second time, there were no hitches. As they set off, however, Joanne could not help remembering the previous occasion when Daniel had given her a lift and wishing that it was Daniel in the car with her now instead of Bernard. Which was a foolish thought indeed, she scolded herself, bordering on the dangerous.

In spite of this wayward thought, the day proved to be a pleasant combination of shopping and sightseeing. Not only did Bernard help Joanne to choose skis and boots with the help of his friend who owned a ski shop, he also took her, after stowing their purchases in the car and having lunch, on a walking tour of the city.

Joanne was fascinated by the miles of arcades with their variety of speciality shops, the historic fountains, the mediaeval buildings, and especially the clock tower with its famous astronomical clock.

'I love ancient towns,' she confided as they strolled beneath the arcade arches, 'especially when they haven't been spoilt. Berne is wonderful, no horrible skyscrapers to ruin it.'

She was not so impressed, however, with the Bear Pit, which they passed on the way to the rose gardens for a view over the town.

'I think it's cruel to keep animals like that,' she said disgustedly. 'Just for stupid people to gawp at and take photographs!'

Bernard was a little taken aback at her vehemence. 'The bear is the heraldic beast of the city arms,' he explained.

'All the more reason to treat them with respect!' insisted Joanne firmly. 'Instead of laughing at them and throwing orange peel. How would you like to be stuck in a concrete pit all day to amuse the tourists?' She directed a quelling gaze on him.

Bernard tucked his arm through hers. 'Perhaps if I were

a bear I wouldn't mind,' he said, 'but I would much rather be with you!'

Joanne walked sadly away and they climbed the hill to the rose gardens.

'It must be very beautiful in spring and summer,' she said, looking at the bare bushes in the intricately laid out beds.

They stood for a time gazing down over the mediaeval town with its spires and red-tiled roofs and bridges over the graceful loop of the Aare. Bernard pointed out places of interest that they would not have time to see on this visit.

'We'll come again in summer,' he promised, 'when the roses are blooming.' And he tangled his fingers lightly in her hair.

Joanne moved away, not sure why she did not want to encourage Bernard. She liked him, but she had a strong feeling that liking was not going to turn to love with Bernard.

By the time they reached the Nydeggbrücke again and crossed back over the river, Joanne was beginning to feel tired and one of her boots was rubbing. It was also colder now.

'I think I'm getting a blister on my heel,' she said, limping a little. She drew her scarf tighter around her neck and pulled up her coat collar.

Bernard insisted she put her arm around his waist for support and he guided her to a cafe for coffee and pastries so that she could rest for a while. Afterwards they drove straight back to Interlaken.

'I hope your blister won't prevent you from going skiing tomorrow,' Bernard said with concern.

As they both had two days in succession off on this occasion, they planned to ski the following day, weather permitting.

Joanne said firmly, 'Nothing will stop me going

tomorrow, Bernard, not if Marie-Claire is still keen. Not if I need a whole packet of Band-Aids!'

'It will be her first outing for a long time,' he said.

'She has to begin some time, and it's better if she begins of her own accord, don't you think?'

'Certainly.' He added rather wistfully, 'We used to go skiing a lot together once. She's a first-class skier. She could have been a champion if she'd wanted to be. She was ski-struck when she met Paolo, and then she was Paolo-struck.' He went on after a moment's reflection, 'She used to paint well too. You must have noticed her pictures in the house.'

'Yes, I have. I've commented on them a few times, trying to arouse her interest in painting again. It's a good therapy, especially for someone as talented as she is. But so far she shows no sign of wanting to take it up again.'

'Daniel's pleased with her progress since you've been there,' Bernard said. 'Nobody had been able to get through to her before. We all tried, all her friends. Daniel even used to take different girls home hoping she might relate better to strangers, but in the end we all had to give up. She just rejected everything and everyone.'

So that was the reason for Daniel's stream of girlfriends, thought Joanne, irrationally relieved.

'Well, let's hope tomorrow provides a turning point,' she said. 'I'm determined to be optimistic.'

She let her gaze drift lazily over the mountains which everywhere dominated the scenery. The sun was low and the valleys drowned in rich purple shadows. The wild rugged beauty of the peaks, contrasting with the neat prettiness of the Swiss countryside at their feet, made it seem almost as though the landscape had been made deliberately soft as a defence against the awesomeness of the mountains. Villages and houses all looked so spick and span and uncluttered, even to the piles of evenly cut firewood in the yards of farmhouses. It was almost as though to be untidy might bring down the wrath of the all-seeing mountains.

'I'm not sure Daniel and Luise really approve,' Joanne said finally. 'I think Daniel is afraid she'll collapse or something.'

'Daniel is naturally very protective. She's his little sister.' Bernard glanced at her, then said slowly, 'Perhaps I should tell you that Marie-Claire and I were once engaged.'

'Bernard! Were you really?'

'Well, there was a tacit sort of understanding. Marriage wasn't actually mentioned, but we seemed to be moving in that direction. Then along came Paolo and Marie-Claire was swept right off her feet. She was in the seventh heaven. I couldn't give her that kind of joy,' he finished wistfully.

'Are you still in love with her?' Joanne asked intuitively.

He hesitated for a second, then lifted one hand from the wheel and placed it firmly on her thigh. 'No, *Liebling*. I am in love with you!'

'I don't believe you!'

'One day I shall muster enough courage to ask you to marry me.'

'Be careful, I might say yes!'

'I shall wait until I'm sure you will want to say yes,' he said, and Joanne felt a sense of relief. She would make certain he never deluded himself to that extent.

A few minutes later, in the deepening dusk, Bernard drove up to the Ahlberg-Peterson house and before she could thank him for the day, he had clasped her face in his hands and kissed her.

Joanne felt her body go rigid. Bernard's lips on hers were almost like a desecration. She liked him, enjoyed his company, but his lips were not Daniel's. Alarmed by this thought, she said hastily,

'Bernard, please—not here. . .'

'It's nearly dark, *Liebling*,' he whispered, 'no one can see us.'

'I must go in,' she protested, and seeing her unwillingness was real, he let her go. 'Thank you for a lovely day,' she added, 'and for helping me buy my skis. I'll see you tomorrow.'

He held her gaze for a moment. 'I wonder if you would be so unwilling if Daniel were to kiss you!'

Colour flamed in her cheeks and her voice was shaky as she retorted firmly, 'What a crazy thing to say! Don't you know that Daniel is practically engaged to Elise Hoffmann?'

'Oh yes, I have heard that,' said Bernard rather dryly.

He carried her new skis and other parcels to the front porch.

'Will you have dinner with me tonight?' he asked, not very hopefully, and with a quirky smile. 'I promise not to make passes at you!'

Joanne almost said yes, but she was tired and her foot was hurting. 'Another time, Bernard. I'm a bit tired tonight.'

He didn't try to change her mind, and quickly left her.

As she was manoeuvring her purchases into the hall, Daniel appeared and startled her.

She said foolishly, 'Hello, Daniel, you're home early,' and instantly realised her mistake.

'I came back yesterday,' he said, somewhat surprised, 'and I've been working at home all today.'

Which she had known he was going to, of course. Joanne felt a complete fool. How could she have said such a stupid thing. She'd seen him at dinner last night, and she was well aware he had spent only two days in the capital this week. What an idiot he must think her!

His look was laconic as he said, 'It would seem your day out has muddled your thoughts somewhat! And confused your memory. Bernard must be a powerful distraction!'

As he spoke, Joanne caught sight of her reflection in the big gilt mirror that hung over the umbrella stand and hall table. She almost gasped. Her hair was dishevelled, her woollen hat awry, her cheeks unnaturally flushed. Probably her lipstick was smudged, although at a distance she couldn't tell. It wasn't hard to deduce what Daniel must be thinking. Oh, why was she always giving him wrong impressions or letting herself down in front of him? It was so infuriating. And especially when the Elsa business was turning out so well, and he had been pleased with the typing she had so far done for him.

While she stood there speechless, he took the skis and ski-boots and said, 'Here, let me. You'll have them all over the floor in a moment. There's no need for you to take it all upstairs, unless of course you plan to have a dress rehearsal in your bedroom or a practice run on the stairs!'

His teasing infuriated her even more. 'Thank you,' she said coolly.

'I'll put yours with the family's skis in the rear porch.' He marched off, leaving Joanne to wend her way upstairs to her room to change for dinner.

She had just showered and was blow-drying her hair when Marie-Claire came in. She looked well-groomed and elegant in a white dress with gold trimming and gold sandals.

'Wow! That's a stunning dress!' exclaimed Joanne. She guessed it would have a Rome or Paris label.

'Paolo chose it,' murmured Marie-Claire, running her palms downs its silky folds. 'It was his favourite.'

Joanne tried not to show her surprise. It was the first time Marie-Claire had mentioned her husband's name.

'It's beautiful,' she said, wondering why the other girl had put it on tonight, but she did not ask since it was her policy not to push Marie-Claire but to let her proceed at her own pace. She said, 'I bought skis and boots today. I hope it will be fine tomorrow.'

She watched Marie-Claire's face anxiously. The girl said, 'Is Bernard coming early?' There was no enthusiasm in her voice, but at least she hadn't changed her mind.

'Yes. He suggested going to Blumenplatz, if that's all right with you.'

Marie-Claire nodded indifferently, then said, 'I want to show you something, Joanne. There is time.'

Joanne tied her robe more securely around her and went into Marie-Claire's room. Laid out on the bed were several colourful skiing outfits.

'Mmm, this one's very dashing!' Joanne exclaimed, lifting the sleeve of an eye-catching suit in black, white and red. The others were vivid yellow and a deep blue and white. 'Which one are you going to wear?'

Marie-Claire shrugged. 'I don't care. I want you to choose the one you like best for yourself. We are about the same size, *ja*? If you go skiing often, Joanne, you will need more outfits.'

Joanne almost fell through the floor. Marie-Claire certainly knew how to startle! 'Oh, but I couldn't. . .' she protested, overwhelmed.

'Please,' Marie-Claire insisted. 'I have many.' She held up the blue one. 'I think this one suits you. *Ja, ist gut!*'

'I don't know what to say,' said Joanne. 'It's very generous of you, Marie-Claire. Thank you.'

'It is new,' the girl said. 'It has not been worn. Paolo and I went skiing a great deal. Look, it is made in Italy. I bought it in Rome—they make such beautiful things at Casa Maggiore. Feel, it is so soft, so warm inside.'

The two girls chatted for a few minutes, while Joanne quickly tried the ski-suit on to see if it really did fit. It did, to both her own and Marie-Claire's delight. Finally Joanne said,

'I'd better go and change. Your mother doesn't like dinner being delayed.'

'Because she's terrified of Fräulein Müller!' returned Marie-Claire, making her first attempt at a joke that Joanne had heard. She added casually, 'I suppose you know Elise and her father are coming to dinner tonight.'

Again she had dropped a bombshell and caught Joanne off guard. Elise! The ballet dancer whom Daniel would probably marry. And she was coming with her father. To Joanne that sounded highly significant. She wished fervently now that she had not turned down Bernard's invitation.

As she squeezed into her grey dress and buckled her patent black sandals, she muttered to herself, 'Don't be stupid! It doesn't matter to you one iota what Daniel Peterson does. He can marry whomsoever he wishes and you couldn't care less!'

'But I do,' she thought with sudden realisation. 'Damn, damn, damn, I do!'

It had been horrible, Joanne decided later in the privacy of her bedroom. The whole evening had been unbearable. And it was her own fault for having fallen in love with Daniel. The culminating idiocy!

It was one piece of idiocy he must never know about, she promised herself fervently. Not in a thousand years would she let him discover that weakness in her.

She was still thinking about the previous evening as she ate her breakfast next morning, reluctantly because she wasn't in the least hungry, and not wanting Elke to be concerned when she came to collect an untouched tray.

If only Elise hadn't been so charming, so friendly, so—so thoroughly nice. Why it would have helped to be able to dislike the girl Daniel was going to marry, Joanne didn't know, but somehow it would have made it easier to bear.

Actually liking your rival was ridiculous!

Joanne sighed over her second cup of coffee. She couldn't even call herself a rival! There wasn't the least likelihood of competition between her and Elise. Elise was beautiful, sophisticated, witty, and famous as well. With Elise to hang on his every word, Daniel was never likely to spare more than a passing glance for a scatterbrained little nurse from England. The fact that he had kissed her once was irrelevant. Dalliance with women was a prerogative some men still believed they had even when planning to marry. She wished she could despise Daniel for it, but you can't despise someone you love!

Elise was not as yet wearing an engagement ring, but Joanne noticed how intimate they seemed and even how close Luise and Herr Hoffmann were. As though they were 'family' already. Joanne had taken to Karl Hoffmann too. He was a surgical instrument maker, managing director of a flourishing international company with an offshoot in England.

Marie-Claire had been almost lively, and once Joanne intercepted a look from Daniel that seemed to convey congratulations. She treasured it as she knew she was going to treasure every little sign of approbation from him from now on. It was gratifying to feel that he was no longer opposed to her being there and tacitly acknowledged that she was helping Marie-Claire, even if only rather slowly.

After dinner, Joanne found herself in conversation with Herr Hoffmann. He asked her about her family, saying when she told him about her father and Terri, 'Gut, Gut—sometimes it does not work, the second marriage. Children can be difficult, especially if they do not have lovers of their own.' He glanced at Elise who was animatedly talking to Daniel. 'I shall be happier when Elise settles down. There was a time when I believed she would sacrifice herself entirely to her career, but love has a way of changing people and forcing them to compromise.' He chuckled softly. 'Luise would like to see Daniel settled too, especially as his first marriage was so tragic. But maybe we cluck too much over our children. Is your father always asking when you are going to get married?'

'No,' Joanne admitted, 'now it's Terri who frets about it. She's so happy, she feels guilty about me!'

When Marie-Claire excused herself, Joanne did likewise, feeling sure that Daniel and Luise would prefer to have the Hoffmanns to themselves. She went straight to bed and tortured herself with images of Elise Hoffmann in Daniel's arms, his mouth hungrily devouring hers.

After she had finished breakfast, there was still time to spare, so Joanne tapped on Marie-Claire's door, with her fingers crossed. There was no answer. Joanne pushed the door open, expecting to find Marie-Claire still in bed, but the sound of the shower told her the girl was up before she noticed the tumbled bedclothes. On the chair lay the black red and white ski-suit. Joanne heaved a sigh of relief. Marie-Claire was still coming.

Before she went downstairs, Joanne risked another quick peep into Marie-Claire's room. Daniel's sister was dressed now and seated at her dressing-table looking blankly into the mirror. Joanne's mouth went dry as Marie-Claire turned round. There was still that dreadful haunted look in her eyes. Joanne expected the worst, but Marie-Claire astonished her by saying,

'*Guten Morgen*, Joanne. I will be ready soon.'

Downstairs, Joanne found Luise hovering anxiously. She pounced on Joanne. 'Is she going?'

'Yes—at least I think so. She's nearly ready.'

Luise was obviously very apprehensive about the outing, although she was trying not to show it.

'It will be better if she masters herself,' Joanne said quietly. 'That's the kind of girl she is, isn't it—normally?

She always fought her own battles and made her own decisions.'

Luise looked startled at Joanne's perception. 'Yes—yes, she did.'

Joanne smiled. 'That's what she's doing now—fighting a battle. I think she'll win it.'

Daniel appeared then and Joanne's heart began its now familiar rapid beating. She looked away from those penetrating eyes, afraid now that he would recognise the longing in hers. Before they had a chance to say more than good morning, the doorbell chimed and Marie-Claire appeared at the top of the stairs.

Luise let Bernard in, and as he came into the hall his eyes went straight to the stairs as Marie-Claire came down. Joanne hadn't expected to see quite so much open admiration in his eyes. He greeted her warmly before he spoke to anyone else.

'*Guten Morgen*, Marie-Claire. *Wie geht es Ihnen?*'

She replied a little stiltedly, '*Guten Tag*, Bernard. *Danke gut, und Ihnen?*'

Bernard turned briefly to greet the rest of them, and Joanne said brightly, 'Well, shall we go?' She felt that although they were skating on thin ice, it was not necessarily going to break.

Daniel came out to the car and helped load the skis on to the roof-rack of Bernard's car. As she was about to get into the car, he laid a hand briefly on her shoulder.

'Have a good day! Don't break any limbs, will you? And especially not your arms! I cannot do without my typist!'

Joanne felt a special kind of warmth suffusing her at his touch and his words, but in the pit of her stomach was the hard knot of truth—all he really wanted her for was her typing!

Luise was standing on the porch, and Joanne felt sorry for her. She would spend a terribly anxious day wondering how Marie-Claire was coping.

Daniel murmured, 'Don't worry. Mama has the utmost confidence in you.'

Joanne was not so sure that he was right. Professionally, perhaps she did, but Luise was Marie-Claire's mother, and that made a difference.

As the car wound its way to the tiny village of Blumenplatz, Joanne tried to take her mind off Daniel by concentrating on the breathtaking vistas of mountains and valleys which spread out all around them as they climbed the mountain road.

She had insisted that Marie-Claire should sit in front with Bernard, and was glad now that she had as she could huddle in the back seat with her thoughts and play only a minor part in the conversation. Marie-Claire was quiet and Bernard did most of the talking, but she did make comments now and then.

Blumenplatz was easily accessible by road, and there were several ski-lifts to the ski-slopes from the village. They paused only long enough to enjoy hot chocolate at the hotel and then set off.

As Marie-Claire had not skied for a year, she was anxious to practise a little, so Joanne decided to leave her in Bernard's care rather than have both of them fussing over her, and risk Marie-Claire being resentful of too much cossetting.

Some good hard skiing on her own, Joanne thought, might help to banish thoughts of Daniel and quell the sudden upsurges of longing she was suddenly prey to. She adjusted her goggles, dug her poles into the crisp snow, then set off on a longish but not too difficult run. When she caught the ski-lift back up again, she looked for another slightly more challenging piste, and caught sight of Bernard and Marie-Claire. She drew an admiring breath. Marie-Claire had not forgotten how to ski!

She was superb.

An hour later they met up. 'Where have you been?' Marie-Claire demanded. Her cheeks were flushed, her eyes bright, and she looked, Joanne thought, like any normal girl having a good time. Perhaps the snow would prove to be her catalyst. Perhaps skiing was the key to her recovery. Joanne fervently hoped so.

'Chatting up handsome instructors!' joked Joanne, and marvelled at Marie-Claire's sudden ability to smile so naturally.

'Did you see Marie-Claire?' asked Bernard proudly. 'She hasn't lost her touch. She can ski anyone into the ground!'

'I know! I couldn't bear to look,' said Joanne. 'I felt so clumsy.'

Marie-Claire just looked embarrassed. Her tension had not quite disappeared, Joanne noticed, but the transformation was nevertheless remarkable.

They set off again and presently Joanne, happening to ski past Bernard and Marie-Claire who were standing still, noticed Bernard bend down apparently to do something to Marie-Claire's boot. As she swished by Joanne heard a peal of laughter and glanced back incredulously. Marie-Claire was laughing! She had sat down abruptly in the snow, her skis awry, her arms flung wide.

As she turned her head again Joanne saw, too late, a figure about to ski across her path. There was no way she could avoid the collision which her foolishness had made inevitable.

A male voice exclaimed angrily in German as she crashed into him and they landed in a tangled heap of arms, legs, ski-poles and skis. Then, after what seemed like a hundred years later, strong arms were around Joanne and a voice was demanding to know if she was all right. He pushed up his goggles and Joanne breathed incredulously, 'Daniel!'

'Good grief! Joanne!'

For a brief moment it seemed that he held her a fraction closer, and she luxuriated in the blissful feeling of lying in the snow cradled in his arms, her body tingling with a surge of extraordinary well-being, until she realised how foolish she was and struggled to extricate herself.

'Are you hurt?' He sounded angry as well as concerned.

'No, I don't think so! I'm so sorry. I shouldn't have looked over my shoulder, but. . .' Couldn't she ever stop making a fool of herself in front of him?

'You idiot!' he exclaimed. 'You could have killed yourself at the speed you were travelling!'

'Yes, I know, but. . .' The words wouldn't come to tell him about Marie-Claire. She could have killed him, she was thinking, or injured him.

Marie-Claire and Bernard came up anxiously. Bernard helped Joanne to her feet. 'Joanne, are you all right? Daniel! What are you doing here? Why didn't you come with us?' He looked perplexed.

'Elise wanted to ski again before she goes off on tour, so we decided to come and find you,' Daniel explained. He struggled to his feet, righted his skis and retrieved his ski-poles.

'Are you all right, Daniel?' Joanne asked anxiously.

He answered rather coolly, 'Perfectly, thanks.'

At the same moment they became aware of Marie-Claire, and Joanne's heart chilled. The hostility in her face was in such contrast to the happy expression of only a few minutes earlier.

She looked at Daniel. 'You came to spy on me!' she spat out angrily. 'You don't think I'm fit to be out on my own even with a nurse and a doctor! Why don't you just have me committed as you want to do and be done with it? You got me off your hands when I married Paolo and you want to be rid of me again. I know what you all want. I know how much easier it would be for you and Mama and Elise and Herr Hoffmann if I wasn't there like a millstone round your necks!'

She paused breathlessly and they looked at her, too shocked by her outburst to react for a moment or two. Daniel recovered first and made a tentative move towards his sister.

'Marie-Claire,' he said gently.

She slid out of his reach and almost collided with Elise, whose cheerful greeting faded on her lips as she saw that something was wrong.

Marie-Claire said in a shrill voice, 'Shall I ski right off the mountain and break my neck? That would solve all our problems, wouldn't it?'

Before they could stop her, she was off down the mountain, skiing towards the village far below.

'After her!' Daniel's face was white with shock and alarm. 'She might do anything!'

It was Bernard who remained cool. He caught Daniel's arm. 'No, you'd better let Joanne handle this.' He rummaged in his pocket and threw a bunch of keys at her. 'In case you need to take her home.'

Joanne could see how desperately he wanted to go after Marie-Claire himself but instead was doing what he thought best. She did not argue and Daniel did not try to stop her going.

Marie-Claire was almost out of sight already and Joanne, still shaky from her fall, knew she would have difficulty catching her up unless she stopped somewhere. Marie-Claire was on the long piste that led right back to the village. Joanne skied as fast as she dared. Bernard's car keys jangled in her pocket and her heart thumped with fear. All at once her ankle began to throb and she realised she must have wrenched it when she tumbled.

By the time Joanne reached the village there was no sign

of Marie-Claire. Joanne mingled with the crowds of skiers looking for her distinctive red, black and white ski-suit, but could not see it anywhere. As she looked out over the valley which dropped for hundreds of feet below the plateau on which the village was built, her fears mounted. There were danger signs in several places beyond the ski-lift station and on the far side of the hotel. There was a safety railing in one place which was a scenic lookout, but further on where the snowfields were unsuitable for skiing, there was nothing to prevent a skier plunging over the edge if one ventured too close.

Suddenly Joanne began to wonder if Daniel had only come because Elise wanted to. Or had he brought Elise as an excuse, because he didn't quite trust her to look after Marie-Claire? Perhaps Luise had even persuaded him to come. No doubt Daniel was cursing himself now for coming, whatever the reason.

'Marie-Claire, where are you?' Joanne cried silently as she looked for telltale marks of skis in the virgin snow near the edge of the plateau. A chough was perched on top of one of the danger signs and it flew off as she approached, a flash of glossy black against the snow, its yellow beak and red legs gleaming in the sunshine.

Joanne was almost in despair when she turned back towards the hotel. Some people were sitting outside in deckchairs and, to her amazement, amongst them she saw Marie-Claire, staring blankly out across the valley and mountains.

Marie-Claire hardly seemed to notice when Joanne quietly crouched beside her and said, 'That was a fantastic run, Marie-Claire. You're a superb skier.'

Marie-Claire turned briefly as though she did not recognise Joanne. She seemed not to understand what she was talking about. Joanne suspected that she might be suffering a memory lapse and that the past few minutes of emotional disturbance had been wiped out.

'It's time for lunch,' Joanne said. 'Shall we go and have some now?'

Marie-Claire shook her head. 'I would like to go home,' she said woodenly.

Joanne did not argue. 'All right,' she agreed. 'Let's go.'

Marie-Claire did not seem to think it odd that Joanne was driving Bernard's car and she didn't even seem aware that they had left the others behind. She seemed almost in a trance. She watched placidly while Joanne fixed their skis on to the roof-rack and then got into the car. She spoke no word all the way back and, after a few attempts at breaking through the almost catatonic state she seemed to be in, Joanne simply let her stare out of the window in peace.

But all the way home she could not help thinking how well the day had begun and how disastrously it had ended. And she could not help feeling that perhaps after all she was as much to blame as Daniel. Marie-Claire had not been up to coping with such a sudden plunge back into real life. Desperately Joanne hoped that all the good work that had been done was not now in vain.

CHAPTER SEVEN

AT DINNER that evening the atmosphere was still very tense. Marie-Claire was in her room, sleeping, and Elise and Bernard had both gone home some time ago. Neither Daniel, his mother or Joanne felt much like eating but were making a pretence of it.

Suddenly Luise, who had been quite calm until now, burst out, 'I knew! I knew something would happen!' She buried her face in her hands. 'We shouldn't have let her go!'

Joanne felt very much to blame. 'I'm sorry,' she answered, and did not dare to look at Daniel. To her surprise and gratification, he leapt to her defence.

'It wasn't your fault! It was mine. *I* shouldn't have gone. I should have anticipated a bad reaction.'

Luise looked at him, stricken, then apologetically at Joanne. 'I didn't mean to blame you, Joanne. It was *my* fault. I made Daniel go…if it was anyone's fault it was mine.'

'Do we have to talk about blame?' Joanne said quietly. 'We all did what we thought was best for Marie-Claire. It was no one's fault really that it went wrong. You couldn't foresee it.'

Daniel pushed his plate aside, the food hardly touched. His expression was wry. 'We ought to be accustomed to setbacks in our profession! There's no easy road to recovery. And sometimes we have to face the fact that there'll be no recovery.' He sighed deeply, and Joanne's heart went out to him with longing to love and comfort.

She said, 'Don't be so gloomy, Daniel. We had a setback today, it's true, but that's all it is.' He wouldn't have been so

108

pessimistic about a patient who was not his sister, Joanne thought.

Luise asked Elke to bring her coffee in her room and she left them straight after the meal. Feeling that Daniel might prefer to be alone, Joanne suggested that she would retire too. It had been a stressful day for them all, but worst of all for her was seeing Daniel's distress and being unable to alleviate it.

He touched her arm. 'No, don't go—not yet.'

When Elke brought in their coffee, Daniel suddenly said, 'Elke, would you mind taking it into the study? No, never mind—give it to me, I'll take it.' He took the tray from her hands and inclined his head to indicate that Joanne should follow him.

When Joanne closed the study door and crossed to the two armchairs with the table between where he had set the tray down and was pouring the coffee, a sudden shaft of pain through her now rather swollen ankle made her stumble slightly and give a little involuntary cry.

Daniel looked round quickly, 'What's the matter?'

'It's all right. I just twisted my ankle when—when we collided this morning. It's nothing.' She grimaced at a fresh jab of pain.

Daniel assisted her into a chair. 'You'd better let me have a look at it.'

'It's just a bit swollen, Daniel. There's no need…I haven't sprained it or anything. It'll be fine tomorrow.' She reached for her cup of coffee, shrugging off his concern.

But Daniel insisted on examining her foot. She winced a little as his firm probing fingers tested the swollen flesh and felt for signs of damaged bones or ligaments. She hoped he was unaware of the alarming effect his touch was having on her and that he would attribute the colour in her face to the hot coffee!

'You need an elastic bandage,' he said, standing up. 'I'll

get one.'

He strode out of the room, returning a couple of minutes later with the bandage. Joanne felt a little embarrassed by all this attention, but it was useless protesting, and it was comforting to have him firmly bandage her aching foot, which he did swiftly and expertly, achieving exactly the right amount of pressure.

'I forgot you were once a GP,' she remarked, and he looked up and smiled reminiscently. He fastened the end of the bandage with a clip and said, 'There, that should help a bit. You'd better keep off it for a few days.' He tucked a footstool under her foot.

'Your coffee's getting cold,' she reminded him.

There was a lengthy silence while he settled into the chair near hers and drank his coffee. Joanne began to feel uneasy. She'd had the feeling he wanted to talk about Marie-Claire, but now he seemed to have changed his mind. She was about to say that she would go to bed when he suddenly spoke.

'I'm sorry you had to bear the brunt of today's little drama,' he said, 'and I want to say again that in no way must you feel responsible. It might have been a big step forward in Marie-Claire's progress if I hadn't intervened. I can't blame my mother. She was worried, naturally, and sometimes personal involvement clouds professional judgement. I don't know what either she or I feared might happen, it was irrational, and I regret it.'

When he paused to refill both their coffee cups, Joanne said, 'It's always easy to be wise with hindsight.'

He shook his head. 'I should have anticipated what happened. I should have guessed she would think I'd come to spy on her. I am aware of her hostility towards her family, and me in particular, after all!' He clasped his temples in his hands and Joanne longed to rush to his chair and soothe with words and touch, but did not dare to. Not being able to comfort him with more than words made her whole body ache unbearably.

Daniel went on in a very low tone, 'She had some reason for what she said, I'm afraid. You see, when she met Paolo, it was a whirlwind romance. She was so young—she's only twenty now.' He sighed deeply. 'My mother and I disapproved of their marrying after only a mere few weeks of courtship. We knew his reputation, we were afraid it would be a disaster, but opposing her only made her all the more determined. She was always strong-willed.' He slanted a faint smile at Joanne. 'We all are in this family! Marie-Claire was determined to marry Paolo. There were bitter arguments and finally she left home. We weren't even invited to the wedding.' He sighed deeply again, and gave her a rueful look. 'You'd think that someone who writes a book for people on how to cope with mental illness in the family ought to be able to handle his own problem!'

Joanne said soothingly, 'Not necessarily. It's always easier to solve other people's problems. The point is that you understand what those problems can be.' She went on, 'Were Marie-Claire and Paolo happy?' She'd had the strong impression from Marie-Claire that she had been blissfully happy. Would Daniel admit that? she wondered.

'Yes,' he said simply, and Joanne admired his honesty. 'You didn't have to be an expert to realise that. We were wrong about Paolo. He ceased to be the playboy he reputedly had been when he married Marie-Claire. When he died, she made us the focus of her grief, as though we were responsible for his death because we'd disapproved. That's why it's been so difficult.'

'Why didn't you let her go to a clinic somewhere away from here?' asked Joanne, knowing that separation from the family could sometimes be the best course to take in cases like this.

'She wouldn't go. She shut herself in her room and refused to see anyone but Fräulein Müller and Elke who brought her meals. I couldn't force her. She's sick, not insane!' Daniel's anguish deepened the lines in his face and Joanne thought how cruel fate was to bring him suffering like this twice in his life. He said, 'It was a major step forward, we thought, when she began to come down sometimes for meals, but that's been, until now, as far as it went. She flatly refused medication of any kind, and became violently upset if it was suggested. Since I don't believe in forcing medication on patients who are unwilling, unless they're dangerous, I didn't insist. I've always hoped that Marie-Claire's cure would come from within herself not out of a bottle.'

'I'm cetain it eventually will,' said Joanne, knowing her words were cold comfort at that moment.

He looked at her steadily. 'I can't thank you enough for coping today the way you did.'

'I didn't do much,' Joanne protested. With a laugh, she added, 'I've often felt that I don't do much more than hand out pills and talk to patients. Psychiatric nursing is different from surgical and medical.'

'And not always as rewarding?'

Joanne shook her head. 'Oh no, it is. I find it very rewarding. It's a branch of nursing that's very special, I think, and I wouldn't want to be any other kind of nurse now. The frustrating part is that people like Marie-Claire need so much more than we can give or even know how to give, sometimes.'

'We're only human,' he said, smiling in an understanding way. 'And there's so much we don't know. Healing minds is not always as easy as healing bodies.'

'Exactly,' Joanne agreed. She smiled. 'Sometimes I feel sure there'll be a big breakthrough in psychiatric medicine one day. . .'

'Like the discovery of smallpox vaccine, penicillin or cardiac surgery?'

She said eagerly, 'Yes. Something you can look at and say, "This is it! this is the big breakthrough we've been waiting for!"'

Daniel laughed softly. 'You're such an optimist! And in case you don't know, talking to you has cheered me enormously.'

Joanne felt closer to him in that moment, both professionally and personally, than she ever would again, she knew. Close and companionable enough to joke, 'Oh—any time you need a therapist!' The sound of his short burst of laughter was her reward, as was the relaxing of the deeper lines in his face. Looking at him now she realised why he was such a good psychiatrist. He was a man who cared deeply, not only for his sister, but for all his other patients as well.

He said apologetically, 'But it's very selfish of me keeping you up so late talking. You must be very tired.'

He was concerned about her too, but that was all it would ever be. Lucky Elise, Joanne thought, to be loved by Daniel. She stood up, gingerly putting her weight on her swollen foot, and found it was scarcely painful at all now.

Daniel rose and took her arm. 'Would you like a sedative? You've had a stressful day and your foot must be giving you some pain. You might find it hard to get to sleep.'

'No, my foot's fine, much better since you bandaged it,' she insisted. 'And I only take sleeping pills *in extremis*, which means for me never!'

He escorted her to the door, stopping there and placing his hands on her shoulders. 'Thank you again, Joanne. . .'

'Daniel—don't. . .' Her eyes stupidly filled with tears as the strain of the day, and now his closeness overwhelmed her. The urge to cling to him and weep on his shoulder was almost irresistible.

He tilted her chin and brushed her lips with his. 'Joanne . . .' It was a tentative, questing utterance of her name and for a mad moment she let him kiss her, luxuriating in the feel of his arms around her, holding her close against him. All her tension seemed to drain away in an instant and she responded to the gentle movements of his lips with soft pressures of her own, unaware that she was conveying more of her feelings for him than she wanted to. Only when he held her more tightly and his kiss became more urgent did she realise what dangerous waters she was sailing into and retreated.

She twisted her mouth away from his, but he did not let her go. His eyes burned into hers, his own feelings unmistakably mirrored in them. 'Joanne...' He clasped her strongly to him, roughly running his hands down her arms, her spine, with a surge of emotional demand that set every nerve in her body a-quiver.

But suddenly she was angry. How dared he trifle with her emotions like this! Did she believe she was the kind of girl he could kiss when he felt like it—when he felt the need for female comfort in times of stress, that he could even seduce her just because she lived in his house? What a pity Elise hadn't stayed for the evening, Joanne thought bitterly.

She pushed him away. 'Daniel, I hardly think this is appropriate! I'm not here to amuse you. I'm here to look after Marie-Claire!' To hide her true feelings she had to be harsh with him.

His shock was profound. 'Joanne! That's monstrous!'

'Yes, it certainly is,' she agreed. 'You caught me in a weak moment, but I promise it won't happen again. Goodnight!'

With a dramatic flourish, she opened the door and limped from the room. She went upstairs as fast as she could, aware that he was watching her, and thankful that he could not see the bitter tears streaming down her face.

Joanne's swollen ankle was much improved by morning, but Daniel and Luise insisted she must rest it for a day at least. When she returned to the clinic, Daniel drove her. He also insisted on redoing her bandage, although she felt it was scarcely necessary any more. As his fingers again examined the now much less puffy flesh of her ankle she thought once again, 'Oh, lucky Elise, to have his kindness and concern for life!'

Finished, he stood up and said teasingly, 'For a nurse, you have quite dainty feet!'

Joanne, relieved that the scene in his study had not caused any lasting awkwardness, took up the teasing and replied with mock indignation, 'A lot of running around doesn't necessarily result in camel feet! Look at ballet dancers!' Then she wished she hadn't said that, because it conjured up too vivid an image of Daniel with Elise.

He chuckled. 'But they get to wear more romantic footwear!'

'Maybe, but I prefer charging around wards in low-heeled lace-ups to tiptoeing about on pointes all my life.' Only when the words were out did she realise he might think she was denigrating Elise, so she added hastily, 'Of course ballet dancing is extremely hard work.'

It was morning coffee break before Joanne managed to speak privately with Bernard. She was alone in the staff lounge resting her foot on a stool for a few minutes while she drank her coffee. He joined her.

'Joanne! What have you done to your foot? Esther said you were in here resting it.'

Joanne smiled ruefully. 'I twisted my ankle when I collided with Daniel. It's nothing. It swelled up a bit, but it's much better today. I'm just swinging the lead!'

He said soberly, 'How is she—Marie-Claire?' Deep personal concern showed in his usually cheerful expression.

'She slept solidly most of yesterday and she wasn't awake when I left this morning. Luise is at home, just in case.' She sighed. 'It was all very unfortunate. You seemed to be getting along so well.'

Bernard slumped into a chair and clattered his mug on the table. He said angrily, 'If Daniel hadn't come—hell, why didn't he have the sense to...'

'Would you have been able to foresee what happened?' Joanne asked quietly. He glared at her. She went on, 'I don't think he really wanted to, but he let his mother persuade him. Don't forget, Bernard—they are involved.'

'Yes, I know.' He was less vehement now. 'But she was enjoying herself so much... And to suggest we weren't competent...'

'I know, it looked that way, but it wasn't Bernard. Luise was worried out of her mind, that's all. She and Daniel are too protective, perhaps.'

He smiled and said, 'You think the sun shines out of Daniel, don't you?'

Joanne went pink. The trouble was, it was so true. Bernard said no more about the incident, but he got up and left abruptly when Daniel came in.

Daniel did not comment on his hasty exit, simply asked, 'Do you feel up to helping me with an ECT treatment? A new client. I want to get started as quickly as possible. She's had the procedure fully explained, of course, but...' He looked down at her and smiled disarmingly. 'She'll need a bit more reassurance, and you do it so effectively. I'd like you to do the pre-med and the pep-talk!'

Scarcely limping at all now, Joanne went along to see Denise, the new client who was, despite reassurances Daniel and the anaesthetist, Alain Lagrange, had already given her, rather agitated. Joanne gave the prescribed injection of atropine and talked to her.

'There's absolutely nothing to be afraid of,' she said, 'and it will all be over in a couple of minutes.'

'I don't like anaesthetics,' Denise confessed, 'and they say shock treatment doesn't work for everyone.'

'No, it doesn't,' agreed Joanne, 'but I'm sure Daniel wouldn't have recommended it for you unless he was quite sure you would benefit from it. He's already explained to you exactly what happens, hasn't he?'

'Yes—he said I might be a bit confused afterwards and have a headache,' the middle-aged woman said nervously. Trying to imagine how it might be had obviously made her anxious.

'And I'm sure he also said that there was nothing to worry about. The confusion will soon pass when you've had a rest and lots of people don't even get a headache.' Joanne smiled at her. 'A little bit of discomfort is worth putting up with to gain a big benefit, don't you think?'

'Oh, yes, of course I do,' said Denise, 'but I'm so nervous about everything.'

'You won't be this morning,' Joanne told her, 'because I'm going to hold your hand and stay with you all the time.'

'Dr Peterson's a very good psychiatrist, isn't he?' said Denise, but unable to completely hide her doubts.

'He's one of the best!' Joanne assured her, and was glad she could say it with complete conviction. 'You can call him Daniel, you know, it's much friendlier. You don't mind if we call you Denise?'

'Oh, no, of course not. It's nice, like a big happy family here. I wasn't expecting that. I thought it would be—well, rather depressing.'

Joanne laughed. 'There you are, you were wrong about that, and you're also expecting ECT will be worse than it really is. I think you're going to be just as pleasantly surprised, Denise, and after the first time you'll be much more blasé about it.'

Joanne held her hand and surreptitiously took her

pulse. It was more normal now. By the time she took Denise along to the treatment room, the new patient was very relaxed and showed hardly any agitation when Daniel applied the electrodes to her head, talking reassuringly to her as he did so.

Before the treatment began, he whispered to Joanne, 'You can sit down if you like.'

'It's all right. My foot's fine now.'

His eyes suddenly held a teasing gleam. 'I wasn't thinking only of your foot. I wouldn't want you to pass out!'

Joanne went bright red. It was the first time he had reminded her of that dreadful first day when she had fainted during an ECT treatment.

'Have I ever done since?' she countered in a low voice, feigning indignation.

'No, but I'm sure if you did, Bernard would be only too happy to fuss over you.'

It was an odd remark, and Joanne glanced at him curiously. Under the apparent humour she had detected an edge to his voice that she had never noticed before.

After the disastrous day at Blumenplatz, Marie-Claire did not mention skiing again, but that seemed to be the only repercussion, apart from the fact that she did not appear to remember the excursion at all. She certainly never referred to it or to her outburst and flight down the mountain.

The days passed much as before with Joanne trying to spend some time each day with her, chatting and having a hot drink around bedtime. Occasionally, if she had been working on Daniel's manuscript and had forgotten the time, Marie-Claire's light would be out when she went upstairs, but Marie-Claire did not seem to resent this.

The girl had again withdrawn into the flat indifference to everything she had shown when Joanne arrived. Joanne tried to stimulate her interest in painting by asking about the pictures which Marie-Claire had painted, but she did not urge her too strongly for fear of producing the opposite result from the one she hoped for. Marie-Claire did show small signs of interest but did not act on them.

Daniel was very appreciative of the typing Joanne did, and greedily took the pages as she finished them. She found it unnerving however, to have to sit in the same room with him as she often did, but she could hardly ask for somewhere private to work. Fortunately, he was not at home every night and when he was in Berne she was able to get on with the work much faster. Once he stood looking over her shoulder as she was typing, which upset her so much she made mistakes.

He rested a hand on her shoulder. 'Sorry, am I putting you off your stroke?'

'Yes, you are,' she replied, trying to control the tremors that his touch sent through her as she corrected the errors.

'I was beginning to think I'd lost the knack!' He chuckled and lightly touched her hair, making her scalp tingle.

Sometimes, she thought, watching him out of the corner of her eye as he returned to his desk, he could be so austere, so distant and unapproachable, and then suddenly he would make a gesture that was warm and human. Touching her was of no special significance to him, of course, but it made her realise what it was like to be jealous. Of Elise.

A couple of weeks later, Esther asked if Joanne would mind doing a spell of night duty. Joanne agreed to, although both Daniel and Luise said she did not have to if she would prefer not.

Night duty, however, offered a welcome break in routine, and it also meant that Joanne could work on Daniel's manuscript in the afternoons when she was fresher than after a long day's shift. She would also see less of him at work and at home, and possibly more of Marie-Claire.

Joanne liked night duty. The calmer atmosphere of a hospital at night was a contrast to the hurly-burly of the day. There was not as much to do, although unexpected crises could always arise, of course. Not that the day shift at the Harder-Kulm was all that frantic. Joanne occasionally missed the more active aspects of a busy hospital with its regular wards, outpatients clinic and community commitments. There were always new ideas floating around at the Barmouth, she recalled with a touch of nostalgia.

After dark, as in many hospitals, the main problem seemed to be patients who had trouble sleeping. Sedatives were used sparingly, warm drinks being a preferred aid to sleep, and often Joanne spent long periods talking to those who could not sleep. Nightmares were sometimes a problem with some patients, and there was one man Joanne had to comfort almost every night, like a child.

Sometimes, when the hospital was very quiet, she would find her thoughts drifting to Daniel, and try as she might she could not distract them. She was always glad when one of the male nurses, Anton, was on duty too, because he liked to play Scrabble and they often whiled away the hours pitting their language skills, sometimes using English words, sometimes German. As a result her German vocabulary improved by leaps and bounds.

One afternoon, after she had woken from a longer than usual sleep and had a very late lunch, Joanne was returning to her room before continuing with her typing for Daniel, when a strange smell tickled her nostrils. At first she couldn't place it, but as she stopped to say hello to Marie-Claire, she recognised it—turpentine. Joanne felt excited as she tapped on Marie-Claire's door.

'Hello. . .' Joanne drew in a swift breath. Marie-Claire

was standing in front of an easel, paintbrush in hand, and on the easel was a large board half covered in bold streaks of paint.

Joanne went into the room and stood for a moment looking at the picture. It was an abstract, but unlike Marie-Claire's other paintings, it had none of the vibrant life they had. It showed definite conflict and drama in a confused way, and in very sombre tones.

Marie-Claire said, 'There are some colours I don't have. Would you get them for me, please, Joanne, next time you're shopping in Interlaken?' She did not seem to be looking for a comment on her work, so Joanne said nothing about it, nor did she say how pleased she was to see the girl painting again. She sensed that it would be best just to accept the fact.

'Of course.' On the spur of the moment she made a change of plan. Daniel was in Berne, so his work was not urgent today. 'I'm going to Interlaken this afternoon to get a few things,' she said. 'Would you like to come with me?'

Marie-Claire wiped her brush on a rag. 'Yes, all right.'

Joanne was glad that neither Luise nor Daniel was at home to be agitated by the outing. In the car, Marie-Claire said, 'You're typing a new book for Daniel?' When Joanne said yes, she was, the girl asked bluntly, 'I suppose he's using me for case material.'

Like so many of Marie-Claire's remarks, this startled Joanne. 'You? I don't think so,' she answered cautiously. Somehow she didn't believe Marie-Claire would have been snooping in Daniel's study.

'What's it about?' asked Marie-Claire.

'Coping with schizophrenia.'

Marie-Claire sighed. 'Again! Daniel is obsessed with it.' Then she asked casually, 'Am I schizophrenic?'

Joanne warned herself to be cautious while still being honest. 'I don't think so.'

Marie-Claire stared out of the window. 'Maybe I am. I'm not always quite myself, Joanne. Sometimes I'm not sure if I'm dreaming, or if I'm dead or alive...and it's horrible...'

It was the first time the girl had spoken about herself so emotionally, and Joanne felt not only a surge of compassion, but also hope. Marie-Claire's acknowledging that she was ill was a good sign.

'Depression affects different people in different ways,' she answered carefully. 'Sometimes it takes a long time to pass.'

Marie-Claire turned to her and said, 'I get so nervous when I go out. I feel people are staring like they did before... when...' She drew in a sharp breath before going on, 'That day we went skiing with Bernard, I got confused and lost my way.'

So she did remember!

'It was a bit confusing for you with so many people around,' Joanne said. Marie-Claire did not, however, show any sign of remembering her confrontation with Daniel.

'Yes, I'm afraid of crowds,' she whispered, covering her face with her hands. 'There was such a huge crowd when Paolo...' Her shoulders shook uncontrollably, and Joanne slowed down so as not to arrive too quickly in Interlaken.

Marie-Claire was, however, quite calm again by the time they reached the town. Joanne's fears that perhaps she had done the wrong thing bringing her subsided. It was quiet in town and Joanne suggested a cup of coffee before they went shopping. Marie-Claire showed no signs of distress, and when they went to the artists' materials shop she became almost enthusiastic, buying much more than tubes of paint.

On the way home she suggested another outing, much to Joanne's surprise and delight.

'You've been here since January,' Marie-Claire declared, 'and you've hardly seen anything, working all the time. We'll go up the Harder-Kulm. You haven't been already?'

Joanne would have denied it even if she had. For Marie-Claire to have taken the initiative was an improtant step and she couldn't help picturing Daniel's face when she told him.

However, after some soul-searching, Joanne decided not to tell him or his mother. If anything went wrong, the responsibility would be all hers; if it didn't, it would be a triumph and both of them would have been saved unnecessary worry.

Marie-Claire proved to be an enthusiastic guide and the trip to the peak of the Harder-Kulm, the mountain nearest the town, was a great success, much to Joanne's relief.

They went up on the funicular railway and had coffee at the restaurant on the peak. After walking around for an hour or so while Joanne took photographs, they walked down to the bottom.

'It will soon be spring,' said Marie-Claire, showing surprising enthusiasm over the swelling buds on the larches and birch trees. 'You'll be able to see the wildflowers on the mountains and go sailing on the lakes. You can take the steamer to Thun.' She added, a trifle downcast, 'We used to have a boat once. I used to go sailing in summer. But everything changed.'

At the foot of the mountain she insisted on taking Joanne to visit the small zoo to look at the ibex, the sure-footed Alpine goat with large curved-back horns, Interlaken's heraldic symbol.

Unfortunately, on their return, both Daniel and Luise had returned early. Joanne's heart sank when she saw Daniel's expression. He was very displeased. Fraulein Muller would have told him where they had gone, of course. But neither he nor Luise said anything until Marie-Claire had brightly told them what a nice day they'd had before she scurried upstairs. When Joanne made a move to follow, Daniel detained her.

Now I'm for it, she thought, nervous but unrepentent.

Luise looked after her daughter, amazed. 'I haven't seen her so animated for a long time!'

Joanne rushed in before Daniel could speak. 'She was fine today.' She twisted the truth a little and told them, 'We just went on the spur of the moment. As a matter of fact, that's twice this week she's been out. She came to Interlaken with me the other day to buy paints. And she wants to take me to the Eiger and the Jungfraujoch on the train. I think it's very promising,' she finished defensively.

Daniel was watching her closely. 'She's painting again?'

Evidently Luise had not told him yet. 'Yes. Rather weird pictures, very dramatic and sombre in tone, but I think it may be a way of working some of the horror of Paolo's death out of her mind. We might be able to gauge her progress from the paintings.'

Daniel scratched his head. His stern expression softened. After a long steady look, he said, 'You seem to be handling her well, Joanne. Thank you.'

If only he would be more than just grateful to her, Joanne thought, but that was the most she could ever expect from him, his gratitude.

That evening, dinner was probably the liveliest meal since Joanne had arrived. Marie-Claire if not bursting with high spirits, was nevertheless much brighter than her usual rather drear, indifferent self. She even directed a question to Daniel, to whom she rarely spoke.

'Have you heard from Elise, Daniel? She's in New York now, isn't she?' Showing interest in another person was unusual.

'Not recently—she's been very busy. It's a hectic tour this time, very gruelling. But Karl says she's well and enjoying herself. She telephones him whenever she can.'

Doesn't she telephone you? Joanne wondered, surprised. Perhaps it was some kind of test of their feelings, not to be in contact directly. Joanne's heart ached, knowing that was probably the case.

'She goes to London next, I believe,' said Luise. 'Karl was hoping to be able to go there to see her at Covent Garden, but his business commitments won't fit in. But you'll be able to see her there, won't you Daniel?'

'I hope so. It's the Foundation's annual meeting shortly.'

Joanne's heart constricted. She chided herself for being jealous, but it was so hard not to be when you loved someone as much as she loved Daniel.

Marie-Claire did not forget the trip to the Eiger which she had proposed, and she surprised Joanne by asking if Bernard would like to join them. He was also surprised, but obviously pleased.

'I think she's jealous!' said Joanne, not entirely teasing.

Bernard gave her a wry smile. 'I doubt it. I was in love with her once, but I would not presume now. . .'

'Bernard,' advised Joanne, 'things often have a way of working out in ways we least expect.'

Spring was definitely in the air when they made the trip. They travelled by train from Interlaken via the picturesque village of Grindelwald to Kleine Scheidegg, where they changed into the train which took them through the long tunnel to the Jungfraujoch. At Kleine Scheidegg, while she was taking photographs of the Eiger, Joanne heard sounds like rifle shots as thawing ice began to crack. Once she saw an avalanche break away and thousands of tons of snow and ice cascaded into the crevasse below. It was an awesome spectacle.

Bernard and Marie-Claire seemed to have picked up the threads of their former friendship, but Joanne did not dare hope that it would eventually blossom into more than that. She was happy to see them laughing together as they slipped and slithered about the Ice Palace in the heart of the mountain. And she was even more delighted when, a few days later, she found Marie-Claire painting a snow scene that was more impressionistic than abstract and had, despite the somewhat threatening aspect of the mountains, a certain tranquillity.

That same day she was in Interlaken buying a few necessities including some paints for Marie-Claire, and posting letters, when she bumped into a man who greeted her with surprise and a warmth that made her look twice at him.

'Guten Tag, meine Fräulein, wie geht's?'

His face and voice were familiar, but it was a moment before she remembered. 'Oh yes, I'm sorry—on the train.' It was the newspaperman who had helped her with her parcels.

'How's the job?'

'Fine, thanks. And you?'

'I was just going to have a coffee. Please join me,' he invited.

As Joanne had been about to do the same herself, she decided she might as well accept. She rather wished she hadn't afterwards, because he seemed to take it as an invitation to become more familiar. He flung his arm around her shoulders as they walked to a cafe, telling her his name was Klaus Reinhardt. Over coffee he invited her to have dinner with him, but Joanne politely declined, saying she was very busy and also on night duty.

When they parted outside the cafe, Joanne looked after his retreating figure with an odd feeling of uneasiness. If ever she saw him again, she thought, she would avoid him completely. There was something about him that made her feel he wasn't to be trusted.

It was a shock when Daniel suddenly appeared at her elbow, emerging, she realised with a little shock, from the cafe where she had just had coffee without noticing him.

'How do you know Klaus Reinhardt?' he asked, with a penetrating look as though she'd committed some crime being seen with the man.

'Is he a friend of yours?'

'No, he isn't!'

'Where did you meet him?'

Joanne told him.

Daniel said, 'Klaus is a shrewd operator. He knows the Harder-Kulm is likely to have clients who might be of interest to his magazine, which specialises in what they call "inside stories" of "human interest" but are really titillating gossip. He has no scruples about invasion of privacy or using the intimate details about the private lives and problems of the rich and famous to boost circulation.'

'I was very careful what I said to him,' Joanne assured him.

'Did he tell you how much he pays for a good story?'

Joanne was shocked. 'Daniel, you're not suggesting. . .'

'Of course not. Just reminding you that you have an obligation to the clinic and our clients. Be on your guard that's all. Klaus is a ruthless journalist.' He took her hand absently. 'I trust you implicitly, Joanne,' he murmured, which made her feel much better.

The next day he asked her to drop what she was doing and type something urgently for him. When she handed the draft he had asked for to him, she said, 'This is your speech for the Foundation annual meeting, isn't it?'

He nodded. 'What do you think of it?'

'It's very interesting. You've certainly got a lot of exciting new plans,' Joanne said admiringly. 'I didn't know you were planning to build a holiday home here in Switzerland.'

'It will be started this spring. I must show you the site sometime. It's near Blumenplatz, a little lower down the valley. It will be in addition to the ones we already operate in England.'

'When are you going to London?' Joanne queried with a pang of jealousy. He would probably come back engaged to Elise.

'Next week,' he told her. 'Which is why this is now rather urgent. I just haven't had time to get down to it before.' He shuffled the sheets of paper that were the draft of his speech and Joanne prepared to go, but he called her back.

'You hear from your father and his wife, I presume?'

'Yes of course. Terri writes long letters full of news and Dad scribbles a bit at the end. They seem very happy.' She could not keep the envy out of her voice, nor ignore the wave of homesickness that suddenly assailed her. She had never been away from home for so long before.

Daniel nodded. 'You must be anxious to see them again, I'm sure. It's time you had a little holiday.'

'Oh, no, I haven't been here long enough,' she protested.

'But you've worked hard, not just at the clinic. We've expected too much of you, I'm afraid. And I wasn't thinking of just a holiday, I have to admit. I was thinking of asking you to do even more work for me. I could do with someone to accompany me when I go to London, to type up notes or letters if I need them. In fact, Joanne, I would very much like you to come with me. You'll have plenty of time to visit your family too.'

Joanne was stunned. It was the last thing she had expected, to be invited to go with him, 'But what about the clinic, Daniel, and Marie-Claire, the book. . .'

He brushed it all aside. 'They can all do without you for a week,' he insisted.

Joanne thought of her father with longing to see him again. 'Well, if you're sure—it would be nice to see Dad and Terri.'

'You have been a little lonely here?' He seemed

concerned.

'No, not really, but I have missed home a bit, I suppose, even though I don't intend to live with them when I go back permanently.'

His eyebrows rose a little. 'You mean to go back eventually? You wouldn't consider staying here permanently?'

'I—I haven't really thought about it,' said Joanne, confused by the steadiness of his gaze, the way he seemed to be trying to read her thoughts. 'My contract is for a year. We'll have to see.'

'Indeed, we shall have to see,' he echoed, and as she moved away, he reached out and gathered her back into his arms. His grey-blue eyes were very searching as he looked into her face and then, perhaps because he sensed her instinctive rigidity, he let her go.

'I'm sorry—I forgot myself. I'm not allowed to take advantage of you in weak moments, am I—or at any other time!'

The mocking tone incensed her. 'No, you're not,' she agreed firmly, while all the time her heart was hammering like a wild thing and she was sure he must have felt it against his own ribs before he let her go.

'Pity,' he said softly, and with a little push, sent her towards the door. 'That's all for today. Thanks, Joanne.'

CHAPTER EIGHT

THE PLANE flew in low enough over the English Channel for the white cliffs of Dover to be sharply outlined against the dark blue sea. As the patchwork of spring green English fields, villages, towns and winding country roads filled her vision, Joanne's throat constricted. She smiled at herself. She had only been away for three months and had not, until this moment, been aware of how deeply she had missed home. Switzerland was beautiful, but it would never tug at her heart-strings as England did.

It was cloudless even over London and Joanne peered eagerly out of the plane window, trying to spot landmarks she recognised. Suddenly Daniel's hand was on her arm, his fingers encircling her wrist. 'Nice to be home again, eh?'

She looked at him a little shamefacedly.

He went on, 'It's home to me too, you know. I was born in England and lived most of my childhood here.'

'I didn't realise that.'

'It was my mother who was always homesick for Switzerland,' he said. 'My father established the Harder-Kulm Clinic because of her. They spent their last years together in Switzerland.'

He squeezed her hand and Joanne could not hide the glitter in her eyes. He would never know that the unshed tears were not so much emotion at coming home, as regret that she would only feel his hand in hers with comfort, never with love.

Less than half an hour later she was hugging her father tightly, then Terri, and introducing them to Daniel.

Andrew Courtney offered to drive Daniel to his hotel, but he insisted on taking a taxi rather than take them out of their way. Joanne parted from him with a pang she couldn't help. She would be seeing him again in a couple of days, but so, in the meantime, would Elise.

'Goodness, isn't the traffic terrible!' she exclaimed as they joined the stream of cars on the A4.

Terri laughed, 'It hasn't taken you long to forget!'

Joanne who, at Terri's insistence, was sitting beside her father, glanced over her shoulder and thought how glowing Terri looked. It still seemed strange to see her father with another woman, but she had felt no resentment, no jealousy. They certainly did seem happy. She couldn't help feeling envious of that.

'We're dying to hear all about everything,' said Terri, and with a meaningful smile, 'especially about Daniel. He's rather gorgeous, isn't he?'

'I thought you were interested in some fellow called Bernard,' put in Joanne's father. 'You mentioned him quite a lot in your letters.'

'Bernard and I are very good friends,' said Joanne. 'And Daniel is in love with a ballerina. You've heard of Elise Hoffmann?'

'My goodness, what elevated circles you're moving in!' exclaimed her father. 'Our lives are going to seem very dull by comparison.'

Joanne had two days with her father and stepmother before she had to go up to London to assist Daniel. She was sure he didn't really need her and that it was just an excuse so she could visit her family without feeling she was being done a favour.

It was a blissful two days and she enjoyed every minute. The only thing that marred her happiness at being home again was thinking of Daniel and Elise. Elise was in London rehearsing and no doubt they were seeing a great deal of each other. Daniel had wrapped tentacles very firmly around her heart and nothing was ever going to prise them away.

On her second morning at home, Joanne went downstairs and found Terri in the kitchen looking ghastly. She was still in her dressing gown and she was nibbling dry toast and sipping Lucozade.

'Terri, what's the matter?' Joanne asked anxiously. Surely she couldn't have eaten anything to upset her? Last night's dinner had been superb and Joanne had no ill effects and presumably neither did her father, since he'd already left for work. Joanne had heard the car drive away.

Terri smiled. 'I'm all right. I'll be OK in a while.'

'You ought to be in bed,' said Joanne. 'You look washed out. Do you want me to call your doctor?'

Terri chuckled. 'Heavens, no! He already knows about it.' She spluttered into her Lucozade. 'Joanne, for a nurse, you're extraordinarily slow on the uptake!'

The penny dropped. With anyone else, it might have been Joanne's first thought, but it simply hadn't occurred to her that Terri might be pregnant.

'You're going to have a baby?' she whispered, dropping into a chair.

Terri looked apprehensive. 'Do you mind very much?'

Joanne was speechless for a moment and then exclaimed, 'Mind? Why on earth should I mind? I think it's wonderful. Great news! Oh, Terri, I ought to have realised . . .'

Terri was smiling. 'I can understand. Actually I wanted to tell you before, but I couldn't seem to get my tongue around it. I hoped Andrew might say something, but he was obviously leaving it to me. I was afraid you might think it was a little—well, infra dig.'

'What! You have to be joking. Why shouldn't you and Dad have children if you want to? I think it's super!'

'I'm so relieved. Andrew's like a dog with two tails. I mean, he's old enough to be a grandfather.'

'He's only fifty-two!' Joanne exclaimed, adding a trifle gloomily, 'And since it's unlikely he'll ever have any grandchildren, he might as well start a second family of his own.'

Terri reached across the table and clasped her hand. 'He'll be so pleased, Joanne. He thinks the world of you, and he feels guilty now for all the years you spent looking after him and not getting married yourself. Is there no possibility this Bernard, or Daniel. . .?' She looked wistfully hopeful.

Joanne shook her head. 'None. Bernard is in love with Marie-Claire, which may come to nothing, but I'm not attracted to him anyway. And Daniel is going to marry Elise.'

'But you are attracted to him,' Terri said, with a level look.

'That's not what I said at all!'

Terri didn't pursue it. 'Oh well, there are plenty more fish in the sea.'

And they can stay there, thought Joanne firmly. Falling in love was too painful, and besides, she knew she would never love anyone the way she had loved Daniel. He was everything she had ever wanted in a man and no man would match up to him, ever.

It was hard leaving her father and Terri, but it wasn't the last she was to see of them. She was to spend the following weekend at home and during the week they were to dine with her and Daniel in London. He had obtained tickets for all of them to see Elise dance in *Giselle*. Terri was thrilled as the Opera House had been booked solid when she had tried to get some herself.

'How wonderful to be able to pull strings!' she exclaimed.

But for Joanne the prospect of sitting beside Daniel watching Elise dance, knowing that his love would be flowing out to her across the footlights and his applause at the end would be straight from the heart, was almost unbearable.

Daniel came down to Blackheath to fetch her in the car he had hired for the week, and she was delighted to find that he got on splendidly with her father and Terri.

That night they dined at their hotel. 'If you've got friends and colleagues you want to see, don't worry about me,' Joanne had said driving up to London.

'I wouldn't be so ungallant!'

'I don't mind being alone,' she persisted, and caught a strange look from him.

Would she really prefer to be alone? he was thinking.

Surely he would rather be with Elise, Joanne thought, sure he was making this gesture out of good manners only.

As a result she felt ill at ease with him at first, but gradually the wine and the good food relaxed her and she soon found herself discussing his book and other subjects of mutual interest with enthusiasm, with Elise firmly relegated to the back of her mind. Just being with Daniel was bliss, providing she didn't dwell on the ephemeral nature of it.

The next day they visited one of the homes run by the Eric Peterson Foundation. It was a special home for handicapped children near Southampton, and Joanne was soon absorbed in the work going on there. She took part in some of the activities while Daniel was conferring with the matron and the medical staff.

It was late in the afternoon when they left and Daniel suggested they stop for a meal on the way.

'I liked the look of that thatched place we passed, the King's something or other,' he said. 'We can have an early dinner instead of a late one back in London.'

'That would be lovely,' said Joanne, adding 'But, Daniel—you had dinner with me last night.'

His eyebrows quirked a little as he glanced at her. 'So? Am I too boring to dine with again?'

'No, of course not! But won't Elise be expecting. . .?'

'Elise is very busy rehearsing and resting in between,' he said with a smile. 'I don't think she would want to dine out with me or anyone.'

Joanne accepted that that was probably true, and in the circumstances she might as well make the most of being a stopgap. She would enjoy little enough of his company alone, and perhaps never as intimately as this again.

'Tell me more about the holiday home you're going to build in Switzerland,' Joanne asked over dinner in the olde-worlde mellow atmosphere of the country inn. 'In the report you said it was not just for children but families too.'

'That's right. In our homes we aim to create a quiet secluded relaxing atmosphere where parents and families with handicapped children can go when the problems get them down. Most don't get a break often enough. It will be primarily for "family therapy", as I call it. We'll have trained staff available, and people will, I hope, form their own self-help discussion groups. But it will also be available for groups of children from time to time. We're going to provide a lot of facilities.'

'It sounds tremendous,' Joanne approved. 'I think parents who cope with handicapped children are splendid, especially the intellectually handicapped. I don't know how they manage.'

'And you a psychiatric nurse!' he said, smiling.

'That's different. Nurses are not personally involved. We can be totally detached.' She added, 'I've never worked with handicapped children. That requires special skills.'

'I'm sure you'd be very good at it. I noticed how well you got on with the children today. You have an instinct for handling people, old or young.'

His warm praise embarrassed her. At least, she thought, she hadn't made a fool of herself recently. She hoped he didn't think her scatterbrained any more.

It was late when they left the inn and they did not talk much during the rest of the journey back to London. Joanne had never felt so companionable with him and she snuggled down in her seat, feeling very close to him, even though she knew she was foolish to indulge her enjoyment of it.

He escorted her to her bedroom door and urged her to have a good night's sleep.

'Busy day tomorrow,' he reminded her.

'Am I to come to the meeting?'

'If you want to. It isn't necessary if you'd rather go shopping. You might find it rather boring.'

'I'd love to come,' she insisted. 'I've nothing to shop for.'

He seemed pleased and mentioned that he might want her to type a couple of letters for him later. Joanne had already checked out the hotel's secretarial service and found that she could borrow a typewriter. She told him this.

'You are efficient!' he said, smiling. He touched her arm lightly. 'Well, goodnight now.' And abruptly he left her.

The next morning Joanne was up early, having slept better than she had expected. Dressed in a neat blue suit with a crisp white frilled shirt and black patent accessories, her newly washed brown hair sleek and shining, she went downstairs to meet Daniel in the lobby as arranged.

'You're looking elegantly executive!' he complimented.

'So are you!' Joanne retorted, laughing as she dared to brush a hair from the shoulder of his dark grey suit.

She was taken aback when he grabbed her hand and held it tightly for a moment, looking searchingly into her face. It seemed as though he was about to say something, but he evidently changed his mind and let go of her hand. Perhaps, she thought, he would really prefer her not to go.

'Are you sure I won't make you nervous?' she asked lightly.

For answer Daniel placed his hand on the small of her back and drew her against him. 'Not nervous,' he said with a throaty little chuckle. And then briskly, letting her go, 'Come on, we're late!'

There were more people at the meeting than Joanne had expected, and Daniel looked pleased at the good turn-out.

On arrival he was greeted by various people and Joanne purposely hung back not wanting to intrude. But he refused to let her simply melt away into the crowd and dragged her forward to meet his friends and colleagues on the board of the Foundation, and their wives.

The meeting was far from boring. Joanne found it lively and interesting and it expanded considerably her knowledge of the Foundation and its activities. She had heard a little about it when she was nursing at the Barmouth and Daniel had told her quite a bit, but she learned much more that morning. She also learned just how highly Daniel was regarded by his colleagues.

Daniel's speech went down well and there was considerable applause for his proposals concerning future directions that the Foundation might take.

'Wonderful man!' a woman next to Joanne murmured. 'So compassionate—like his father. And handsome with it!'

Joanne felt enormously proud.

A buffet lunch was served in an adjoining room and during it she found herself talking to a number of different people and even heard herself boldly expressing opinions on mental health care, afterwards being astonished at her temerity. She was so afraid of letting Daniel down.

When she prefaced one remark with the words, 'Well,

I'm only a nurse...' the eminent psychiatrist who had asked her opinion frowned disapprovingly.

'Only a nurse?' he queried. 'My dear Miss Courtney, without nurses where would we be? Psychiatric nursing requires a very big commitment and a constantly positive attitude as well as compassion of the highest order. A good nurse can learn more about her patients and their disorders than anyone sometimes. Nurses' observations are very vital indeed.'

'Joanne has an intuitive approach which sometimes works little miracles,' murmured Daniel, and unseen by the others, he slipped his arm around her waist. Joanne flushed guiltily.

Later, returning to their hotel in a taxi, he said teasingly, 'You certainly found a champion in Sir Edwin!'

'I was terrified of him!' she confessed. 'He looks so formidable with those black eyebrows twitching at you.'

Daniel laughed. 'Old Edwin! His bark is worse than his bite.'

'Like yours,' said Joanne—and bit her tongue. It was such a silly remark, but silly remarks had a habit of slipping out when she was with Daniel.

He was sharp. 'Is that what you think?' He'd never thought of himself as formidable, and it was a shock.

Joanne tried to wriggle out of it. 'Well...' But he wouldn't let her. 'You find me intimidating?' He looked quite hurt.

They were held up at the traffic lights in heavy traffic, and impulsively Joanne touched his arm. 'No, of course not—not now anyway, but at first you were—a little.' She smiled at him impishly. 'You didn't approve of your mother employing me, remember? And I did keep doing stupid things in front of you. You must have thought me an impossible idiot.'

He looked aghast, then caught hold of her hand and enveloped it in his large palm. 'Joanne...' The grey-blue eyes were full of apology. 'I'm sorry, But truly, I never, I'm quite sure, thought you an impossible idiot!'

'Oh, yes, you did,' she said mischievously. 'I heard you tell your mother that I was a bit of a scatterbrain and probably unsuitable and unlikely to be any help to Marie-Claire.'

Daniel's face was a picture of dismay. He was remembering. 'Oh dear—you overheard me say that, did you? Yes, well, I suppose I shall have to admit it. Perhaps you did seem a bit—well. . .'

'Irresponsible.'

'Hardly that! But. . .' he floundered.

'*Flatterhaft*?' she suggested slyly, and they both laughed.

Whether it was the fault of the taxi starting off again with a jerk Joanne couldn't tell, but suddenly her palm was against his lips and he had turned to her and with warm fingers spread against her cheek, made her look at him. Then he lightly kissed her lips.

'Daniel, we're in the middle of Piccadilly!' she protested.

'So what!' he whispered, and kissed her again. Then, smiling at her confusion, he sat back and said, 'Thank you for coming today. It was good to have moral support.'

Which he hadn't needed in the least, Joanne knew. He was just being kind. How much happier he would have been if it had been Elise at his side. The kiss meant nothing. Daniel was just saying thank you in a flirtatious way, that was all. It meant nothing to him, but it meant the whole world to her.

Elise was not at Daniel's side that evening, but she was not far away. After an early dinner at a nearby restaurant, Joanne and Daniel accompanied Andrew and Terri Courtney to the Opera House. There was a wonderful air of excitement as it was the opening night of *Giselle*.

Joanne was pleased that her father and Daniel seemed to get on so well, despite their differing professions. They

were still talking animatedly when the party entered the
theatre. Terri and Joanne amused themselves taking note
of the fashions in the audience milling around the foyer.

'I love Covent Garden!' exclaimed Terri as they found
their seats in the stalls, in an excellent position near the
front. 'All this red plush and gilt, it's so theatrical and
romantic!'

Joanne agreed, but she could not take the same pleasure
in it all because of the ache in her heart. Elise's
performance as Giselle was magical, and glancing
occasionally at Daniel beside her, Joanne noted a rapt
expression. His applause was loud and enthusiastic, and
along with many others he was on his feet shouting 'Bravo!'
at the end.

The applause was tumultuous and Elise took many
curtain calls, coming back again and again, alone and with
other members of the cast, and looking, Joanne thought,
so sparkling, she must be in love. When a page brought
Elise a huge bouquet of roses and she blew a kiss into the
audience, Joanne felt sure she knew who had sent the roses
and for whom the kiss was intended.

'Wasn't she wonderful!' Terri enthused as they began to
move out of the theatre.

'Magical,' replied Joanne, meaning it. It was the best
performance of *Giselle* she had ever seen, and Elise
certainly deserved the title of prima ballerina. But never
had she felt so leaden in her heart.

Joanne would have liked to have gone back to the hotel
after the performance, but they were invited to a party with
the cast and to plead a headache or other indisposition
might have looked too obviously like an excuse. Joanne
did not want anyone—and Terri was perceptive—to guess
how she really felt about Daniel. Besides, she could hardly
abandon Terri and her father.

The party was very crowded and Daniel, Joanne

noticed, seemed to be having a problem getting anywhere near Elise, who was besieged by well-wishers. But when the fuss was all over, then they would be alone. And perhaps tomorrow they might even announce their engagement.

Andrew Courtney was concerned about Terri overdoing things, and when he whispered to Joanne that he thought they would slip away soon, Joanne said she would leave with them. It would save Daniel having to get a taxi for her or arrange a lift.

Terri was not keen on being fussed over, however. 'I'd just love to meet Elise,' she said wistfully, and leaning back against her husband, she added, 'If it's a girl, can we call her Elise?'

He folded his arms around her waist. 'Why not?'

Joanne felt a sharp pang of envy for Terri and her happiness and marvelled at how much younger her father suddenly seemed.

He was just saying, 'I don't think you'll have much of a chance, love, unless you shove through the throng,' when Daniel joined them with Elise in tow.

She stayed talking to them for some minutes, asked if they had managed to get some supper in the crowd, and was as sparkling and fresh as though she had not just danced a gruelling role in front of hundreds of people.

When the conductor, Josef Baumgarten, appeared at her side and whispered that he wanted her to meet someone, she gave a brilliant smile and clasped his hand, introduced him to the others and then, or so it seemed to Joanne, exchanged a secretive little smile with Daniel.

Joanne was therefore astonished when she said, bending close to him, 'Thank you, Daniel—thank you for everything, and especially your patience,' then melted back into the crowd with the conductor.

Andrew said they were leaving and Daniel astounded

Joanne by grabbing her arm and saying, 'Let's get out of
here too, shall we?' before she had a chance to say she was
going with her father and Terri.

'But don't you want to stay?' faltered Joanne.

He shook his head. 'No. I hate parties But this was
Elise's big night, and I promised to come. Come on, let's go
before all the taxis disappear.'

They walked with Terri and Andrew to their car and
then Daniel hailed a cab. Joanne could not understand it at
all. Was his not hanging around during the celebrations
part of a compromise? Daniel obviously did not feel
comfortable in the limelight, but it still seemed strange to
Joanne that he had not stayed tonight of all nights.

'Nightcap?' he asked when they reached the hotel foyer.

Joanne did not want another drink. She'd already had
several at the theatre party, but despite all the sensible
voices that told her not to, she wanted to stretch out being
alone with Daniel a little longer.

'If you're having one,' she said, wondering why she was
so willing to torture herself.

They sat in the lounge and talked about the ballet and
Elise's triumph and then about Joanne's father and Terri,
but Daniel seemed preoccupied and Joanne felt sure he
was wishing he had stayed at the party after all.

When Joanne stifled an involuntary yawn, he said, 'Do
you know what time it is?'

She glanced at her watch. 'Two a.m.! I hadn't realised.'

They went up in the lift together and outside Joanne's
room, Daniel paused.

Joanne said, 'Thank you for this evening, Daniel. For all
of today. And thank Elise again for getting tickets for Terri
and Dad as well as me. It was very kind of her.'

He was gazing down at her and Joanne felt a shiver run
through her. She looked away and was about to insert her
key in the door when he took it from her and opened it

himself, swiftly pulling her inside and closing the door behind them before she could even utter an exclamation.

'Daniel. . .' she whispered now in the dark, utterly perplexed.

He murmured huskily, 'I'm going to kiss you properly, Joanne, in private, whether you like it or not!'

'But. . .' she began feebly.

Her protest was buried in the gentle warmth of his lips on hers. He held her close and she melted under his strength willingly. There was no way she could prevent the upsurge of deeply hidden feelings that his nearness aroused. She swayed against him and responded to his kisses with an abandon which might have appalled her if she hadn't loved him so much. That he assuredly loved Elise had no meaning at that moment.

Her handbag slid to the carpet, and when he picked her up and carried her across the room to the bed, she did not resist. Her shoes fell off as he laid her gently on the bed and she saw his face dimly in the glow of London lights through the undrawn curtains. He cradled her in his arms as though she was all the world to him as he was to her.

'Joanne—*meine Leibling*,' he breathed softly. 'I need you so much. . .'

Joanne caught her breath. The full impact of her madness in allowing such a situation to develop hit her like an avalanche of snow. She eased herself away from him and lifting his hand which softly stroked her thigh, held it momemtarily. 'Daniel, I think you'd better go,' she said quietly but firmly.

'Why?' He clutched her hand tightly. 'Why do you tantalise me and then. . .'

'Daniel, I'm sorry. I got a bit carried away too, but I don't want to be a partner in a last-minute pre-marital fling.'

He dropped her hand as though it had burned him. 'What are you talking about?' He reached over and switched on the bedside lamp, looking incredulously into her flushed face.

'Elise,' she said reproachfully. 'You're going to marry Elise, aren't you?'

'Marry Elise? What gave you that idea?' he demanded grimly.

Joanne said defensively, 'Most people expect you to.'

Daniel snorted. 'People love to gossip!'

'But you are, aren't you?' she insisted.

'No, of course I'm not!'

Joanne was wandering in a maze. 'But you were seeing a lot of her when she was home, and your mother said. . .' she floundered. 'And tonight—the roses, the kiss she blew you.'

He laughed suddenly. 'The roses were from Josef! The kiss was for the conductor, the man Elise is going to marry. They intend to make an announcement at the end of the season.'

Joanne could not deny the possessive way the conductor had taken Elise away. 'Is that true, Daniel?'

'Yes, *Liebling*, perfectly true. Didn't you notice how she sparkled tonight? It wasn't just her success as Giselle. The girl's in love. Now, look at it sensibly. What sort of marriage would Elise and I have? We'd always be apart. It wouldn't work. With Josef she has a partner who shares her career, they can travel anywhere together. Shall I tell you a little secret? They'd quarrelled a while ago. Elise was suffering from overwork and stress and was unsure of herself. So she came home and refused engagements for a couple of months. I was sort of honorary psychiatrist, you might say. She eventually decided she did want to marry Josef.'

And not Daniel, thought Joanne, believing she now understood. Elise had turned Daniel down. That was why he hadn't wanted to hang around tonight. That was why he was here with her now, trying to obliterate his true feelings by seeking comfort in the arms of another woman.

His lips brushed hers. 'Kiss me, Joanne...' And she did, because she couldn't stop herself.

She quivered to the gentleness of his touch as he pushed the straps of her dress off her shoulders and buried his face in the soft warm hollow of her neck and cupped a hand around her breast, and she knew she had a chance to bind him to her now. She could take what Elise didn't want. Daniel would make love to her tonight, and on other nights, but would he marry her? Would Daniel Peterson, eminent psychiatrist, marry an ordinary little nurse from his mother's clinic? They came from different worlds, and in her heart Joanne knew she could not fool herself that he would want her to share his as his wife.

With a supreme effort of will, she pushed him away. 'No, Daniel,' she said in a weary tone. 'Don't...'

He raised himself on his elbows and looked into her face, with longing and puzzlement. 'Joanne, what's wrong? You seem so responsive one minute, and then.. Joanne, I won't force myself on you—just let me stay with you—please!'

'No, please go,' she said, struggling to keep the tears from falling. 'I don't want you to stay.'

He caught her chin roughly between finger and thumb and made her look at him. 'Is there another man, Joanne? Bernard?' A harshness made his voice gritty.

'No!' she denied sharply.

'What about that crummy journalist, Klaus Reinhardt?' His scorn seared her. How could he even think she would befriend Klaus Reinhardt?

'Please, Daniel, does this have to turn into an inquisition?'

'Not if you tell me why you find my advances so repellent.'

'I don't. . .' Joanne swallowed hard. There was no

alternative but to lie to him. He would never admit that he only wanted her because Elise had rejected him. So she said dully, 'There's a doctor I used to go out with before I went to Switzerland. He went to Canada—he'll be back soon.'

Daniel looked stunned. She had evidently given it a ring of truth.

'I see. It's a pity you didn't tell me that before. But you let me think…' There was deep reproach in his voice, and hurt pride too. Joanne felt guilty. But she couldn't—no, she couldn't let him make love to her when she knew he would never love her as she loved him.

'We're all human,' she muttered. 'We all get carried away sometimes, don't we?'

With an ironic twist to his mouth, he said, 'Yes, Joanne, I suppose we do. I'm sorry, it won't happen again.' He added, 'Sleep well,' and was gone swiftly and silently from the room.

Joanne knew she would be unable to sleep a wink in what was left of the night.

CHAPTER NINE

JOANNE contemplated their return to Switzerland with mixed feelings. One part of her wished she could remain in England and never see Daniel again, but the other, more foolish part of her insisted that half a loaf was better than none and that a relationship based on friendship and professional interests would have its own rewards. She did not hope that he would fall in love with her. That would have been presumptuous.

The weather, which had been fine over most of Europe for the past week, changed dramatically just before they left London. Winter came back with a vengeance. Storms and blizzards swept across the Continent and even brought late snow to London. There was snow on the runway when their plane took off from Heathrow, and it was snowing when they arrived at Zurich and caught a connecting flight to Berne.

Daniel seemed preoccupied and said very little on the journey. Believing she knew the reasons why, Joanne did not attempt to make small talk. She had spent the last two days with her father and Terri, during which time she had managed to divert her thoughts from Daniel temporarily so that they did not suspect the turmoil beneath her cheerful exterior.

She had returned to the hotel for the last night of their stay, to find that she and Daniel were invited to dine with Elise and her fiancé and other members of the ballet company. It had been a sparkling evening, despite some nervousness on Joanne's part, and had been marred only by the irony of Elise's rather naive assumption that Joanne and Daniel were more than just good friends. Didn't she realise how heartbroken he was? For the first time Joanne came close to disliking Elise.

On the plane, Joanne tried to read a novel, but found it hard to concentrate. She was too acutely aware of the constraint between them because of her rejection of him the night they had been to the ballet, and being so close to him kept her nerves on edge.

When he put down his medical journal and spoke after a long silence, Joanne jumped. 'Good story?' he queried. 'Must be—you were lost in it!'

She had been lost in her thoughts, not the story, 'It's not bad,' she said.

Daniel clasped his hands behind his head and yawned, stretching his feet as far as they would go under the seat in front. His journal slid on to the floor. Joanne retrieved it and stowed it in the pocket of the seat in front.

'Aren't you tired?' Daniel enquired. 'It was a hectic week with quite a few late nights.'

'I enjoyed it,' she said. 'I don't feel a bit tired.'

'I suppose it was a bit hard leaving home again.'

'It was lovely to see Dad and Terri, of course, but I'm looking forward to getting back to the clinic. I wonder how Elsa is coming along. And I hope Marie-Claire has been keeping up with her painting. I managed to get all the paints and special brushes she wanted.'

Daniel smiled at her. 'It was good of you to go shopping for her.'

'I'm finding it fascinating. I might take up oil painting myself one of these days.'

He picked up his magazine again and Joanne returned to her novel, but turned the pages without really taking in what she was reading. She was glad it was only a short journey.

There were no delays and they arrived in Berne on time, to be met by Luise. She welcomed Joanne so warmly it was almost like coming home to a second family.

'We've missed you,' she said. 'Marie-Claire especially. Although I'm pleased to say she has been out once, skiing with Bernard. She seemed to enjoy it.'

Joanne and Daniel agreed that that was good news.

The following night Joanne went back on duty. As she still had some typing to finish for Daniel on the new book, she was happy to stay on night shift for the time being, for which Esther was grateful.

Joanne had been pleased to find that Marie-Claire was more relaxed and inclined to talk more. Marie-Claire was delighted with the art materials Joanne had brought from London and she was also eager to hear about the trip and asked a lot of questions about Joanne's family.

'I wish I could have gone to the ballet!' she said wistfully. 'And I can't remember when I last had dinner in a restaurant.'

The fact that she seemed to be missing that part of her former life was encouraging. Joanne suggested casually, 'Why don't we ask Daniel and Bernard to take us out to dinner some time?' She felt guilty for suggesting it, because it would give her a chance to be with Daniel.

But Marie-Claire was reluctant to commit herself to a definite arrangement. 'Some time—maybe,' she said evasively.

Joanne did not pursue it but reminded herself to mention the idea to Bernard. It seemed obvious that their friendship was blossoming again, and it might be that Bernard would prove to be the vital ingredient in Marie-Claire's rehabilitation. Joanne hoped Marie-Claire would not break his heart this time.

When she talked to Bernard about Marie-Claire, he said, 'She almost began to talk about the accident the other

day. I led her as gently as I knew how, but she suddenly
clammed up on me, so I left it at that. It was a good sign,
though.'

Joanne nodded and smiled understandingly. 'I think
you're good for her, Bernard. What she needs is expert
psychotherapy, but she has always refused any treatment
at all. You can give it to her informally without her realising
it.'

'I'm trying,' he said, and Joanne was sure from the look
in his eyes that he was in love with Marie-Claire all over
again.

As for her own situation, she had worked out the
immediate future. As soon as Daniel's book was finished,
and Marie-Claire no longer needed her, she would find
alternative accommodation. She would work at the clinic
until the end of her contract and then she must try and find
the will to leave. However precious were the moments she
shared with Daniel, she would be foolish to let him rule her
life. Daniel would marry someone else one day. It must be
possible to get over loving someone, she thought, if you
really tried. He would get over Elise, so surely she would
get over him in time. Terri's baby would be due about the
same time as her contract ended. It would be nice to be
back home then.

On her second day back from London, Joanne ran into
Klaus Reinhardt again, and in much the same way as
before. She was in Interlaken shopping with Marie-Claire
whom she had left in the art materials shop while she went
to the post office, arranging to meet her at the duckpond in
the main street.

Joanne arrived first and paused to watch the ducks. As
two of them took off and flew at low level along the street
and turned left to the lake, she heard someone call her
name.

'Joanne! *Guten Tag*!' His hand gripped her sleeve and

she turned round, startled. She was dismayed to see who it was.

'Oh, hello, Klaus,' she said without enthusiasm.

'I have been hoping to see you,' he said, his eyes flirting with her. 'I telephoned the Harder-Kulm Clinic, but they told me you were in England.'

'How did you know I worked there?' Joanne asked sharply.

'It is my job to find out things!'

'What did you want?' she asked, annoyed that he should have sought her out. She had been offhand with him before, hoping he would take the hint and accept that she was not interested in him.

'I thought we might meet as I was home for a while,' he said blandly.

Joanne ignored that. 'I'm sorry,' she said, 'I'm in a bit of a hurry. I'm meeting someone.'

'Will you have dinner with me?' he persisted.

'Thank you, but I'm afraid I can't. I'm still working nights.'

'Surely you have days off sometimes?' he queried.

Joanne was beginning to feel annoyed with him now. 'Yes, of course I do, but I—er—have a regular arrangement.' She hoped he would assume she meant with a man. A short way along the street she spotted Marie-Claire walking towards them. 'I must go now, Klaus. I'm meeting a friend.'

Klaus, however, did not let her go easily. He fell into step beside her and as Marie-Claire came up to them, smiling he said, 'May I take you and your friend for a cup of coffee?'

Marie-Claire was looking curiously at Klaus, but Joanne was determined not to introduce her. 'No, thank you, Klaus,' she said firmly. 'It's kind of you, but we're in a bit of a hurry.'

She hustled Marie-Claire away as quickly as she could, and drew a sharp breath of relief. Had Klaus recognised her? If he had he was bound to be hot on her trail. Maybe that was why he was in Interlaken, she thought. Daniel had warned that there might be an upsurge of interest when it got close to the anniversary of Paolo's death. There were magazines, like the one Klaus worked for, who would like to run an exclusive story about Marie-Claire then.

'Who was that man?' Marie-Claire asked when they were in the car.

'Oh, just a man I met on a train,' said Joanne. 'He's twice tried to make a date with me and I've rebuffed him, but he doesn't take no for an answer.'

'You don't like him?'

'No, not very much.' Joanne did not tell her why. If Marie-Claire thought journalists were after a story about her, she might retreat very promptly into her shell.

'I'm glad.' said Marie-Claire without giving a reason, and when Joanne asked why, she just shrugged and smiled and refused to say.

The wintry weather continued despite the fact that it was spring. The green mountain pastures disappeared under a blanket of snow again, farmers led their cows back into the byres, and ski resorts stopped planning their own holidays and made the most of a late influx of skiers.

Joanne did not see much of Daniel, which pleased her on the one hand and made her ache with longing on the other. She felt desolate without him, but disconcerted when he was there. She had almost finished typing the manuscript and in some ways she felt glad about that, even though it had been a kind of bond between them. She must concentrate on overcoming her deep feelings for the man, she told herself, while knowing that it was unlikely she ever would.

One evening at dinner Marie-Claire said she and Bernard were going skiing again and invited Joanne to come too. Then, surprisingly, she said to Daniel, 'You said some time ago you would show us the site for your holiday home, Daniel. It's near Blumenplatz, isn't it? Why don't you come and make a foursome, and we can all see the site.'

Daniel did not show how surprised he was. He simply said, 'Why not? Let me know when you plan to go.'

A few days later the planned excursion took place. The weather was still wintry, but there were signs of thaw. Bernard said, 'I don't think we've quite finished with winter yet. It's just one of those years.'

They went to Blumenplatz and on the way stopped off so that Daniel could show them the site for the planned holiday home which the Foundation intended to build soon.

'There'll have to be considerable landscaping,' Daniel explained. 'And we plan to have a heated swimming pool and sauna, tennis courts and many other facilities for summer and winter sports. We'll be able to accommodate about twenty people at a time in ten units. That's not many, I know, but there's plenty of room here to expand later.'

'It will be a wonderful place for people to come to, to get right away,' said Joanne approvingly. 'The mountains are very relaxing.'

Bernard too was very interested in the project and Marie-Claire asked questions about it, showing an unexpected interest. Joanne was delighted with her progress and she hoped fervently that nothing would happen to mar their day this time.

It was a beautiful clear day with blue skies and brilliant sunshine, and at Blumenplatz there were quite a few people sitting outside on terraces or on the snow in deckchairs, making the most of the balmy atmosphere. The village was not as crowded as it had been previously, but the ski-lifts were all busy and the lower slopes were also popular.

They stayed near the village until lunchtime and then after a meal at the hotel, took a ski-lift higher up. A few clouds were scudding across the blue now and there was a wreath of misty cloud around the distant peaks of the Eiger and the Jungfrau. Marie-Claire was in excellent spirits and seemed happy to give most of her attention to Bernard. There would be no catastrophe today, Joanne thought with relief.

After their first couple of runs, Marie-Claire said she wanted to try one of the more difficult pistes, so she and Bernard went off together.

'See you back at the hotel,' said Bernard.

Joanne did not feel competent to tackle the more difficult runs, so she said to Daniel, 'Don't let me hold you back. I'll be all right.'

He shook his head. 'This area suits me too. Besides, I don't want to butt in.'

Joanne knew he was remembering how disastrous his butting in had been once before and he naturally wasn't going to risk any misunderstanding today.

'It's nice to see Marie-Claire looking so happy,' she said.

Daniel's eyes met hers. 'She's come a long way since you've been with us. Not so long ago she wouldn't even see any of her old friends.'

'Bernard is doing more than I ever could, Daniel,' Joanne pointed out.

'Yes, but if it hadn't been for you, he wouldn't be! You have a knack of making things happen. Look at what Marianne is doing for Elsa.'

'Yes, I'm pleased about that,' said Joanne. She was also relieved that her plan had worked.

Daniel said, 'Elsa's whole outlook has changed. I've talked to her parents and they've agreed to let her go to

Paris with Marianne for a while. Marianne has decided to set up her own agency and gradually retire. They've helped each other.'

'Was it difficult talking Elsa's parents round?' asked Joanne. 'They sounded pretty formidable to me.'

'They were! But I managed to convince them, and of course Marianne is so well known and highly respected, they could hardly find fault with her taking Elsa under her wing.'

Joanne laughed. 'I bet your powers of persuasion had most to do with their changing their outlook!' She glanced up at the sky. 'Talking of outlooks—it's clouding over.'

Daniel squinted at the sky. 'We'll have more snow tonight, I reckon.'

They skied for another hour and then the weather suddenly began to close in. An icy wind whirled snow across the slopes and skiers began to head back to the village via the slopes or on the ski-lift.

'I wonder where Marie-Claire and Bernard are?' Joanne said.

'They'll go down when they see how the weather's turning,' Daniel assured her. 'Come on, we'd better get moving.'

'Yes, this wind is bitter,' she agreed.

'Shall we take the ski-lift?'

Joanne nodded. She was beginning to feel tired and they were quite a long way from the village. They squeezed into the seat on a ski-lift, and a tremor ran through her as Daniel slid his arm around her shoulders.

Back at the village, they stowed their skis on the roof-rack of Bernard's car and then strolled along to the hotel. As their skis were not already on the car, Marie-Claire and Bernard were evidently not back yet.

'They'd better hurry,' said Joanne. 'It's starting to snow, and you can scarcely see the higher slopes now.'

Daniel frowned slightly. 'They're both experienced skiers,' he said. 'They'll have started down as soon as the weather started closing in.'

Joanne noticed the forest of skis outside the hotel. 'Perhaps they're already inside.'

But Marie-Claire and Bernard were not in the hotel bar where they had arranged to meet. Joanne felt a twinge of anxiety and she was sure Daniel felt uneasy too, although he had said nothing. They would be both relieved when the other two arrived back.

Joanne found a table near a window and Daniel brought her a cup of hot chocolate. She must have been looking worried, because he said, 'Bernard wouldn't take any risks.'

Joanne looked up the mountain behind the village. Visibility was diminishing fast and the light was fading as the snow clouds swept in low over the mountains. People were now crowding into the bar and through the window Joanne could see more arriving back from the ski-slopes, but no sign of Marie-Claire and Bernard.

'I wish they'd hurry,' she said, speaking her thought aloud without realising it. 'It's getting awfully dark.'

Daniel's hand rested over hers. 'Don't worry. . .'

She looked at him. 'Will we be able to see our way home if the snow doesn't stop?'

Daniel started to answer her, then paused and they both listened. At the same instant a hush fell over the bar as everyone else heard it too.

'Is that thunder?' Joanne was never sure whether she actually spoke the words or merely framed them in her mind. All she could remember later was that from where she was sitting she saw half the mountainside break away— or so it seemed— and begin its horrifying slide downwards.

'Daniel!' she screamed, leaping up, but her voice was a pitiful squeak as she flung herself into his arms.

Daniel saw it too and shouted, 'Avalanche!' but the word was buried in the deafening roar that obliterated all other sounds even the shrill screams of the skiers in the crowded hotel bar.

The lights went out and in the gloom Joanne saw nothing and felt nothing except a blast of cold air and the hardness of Daniel's shielding body as he pressed her against a far wall. A wall of snow tore down the front of the hotel with a sickening crunch and buried the very spot where they had been sitting under tons of snow.

'Oh, my God, Joanne. . .' Daniel's voice was filled with horror as he held her tighter and tighter and the snow sprayed over them. 'Joanne—my love—*meine Liebling*. . .'

Joanne closed her eyes and waited for them to be buried alive. At least she was with Daniel. She was in Daniel's arms at the end.

But there was no more snow, only the drifting snowflakes that swirled in under the shattered hotel roof. They blew into Joanne's face and she tasted cold crystals on fear-dried lips. Daniel's grip did not ease for some seconds, then he looked down at her. 'Are you all right?' He sounded as astonished as she felt to find that they were still alive.

'I'm fine,' she replied shakily, her teeth chattering.

They dared to look around, still too numbed to move. But as they moved so did others who had escaped being buried. Voices shouted urgently, cried out for help, and for some time there was confusion and occasional outbursts of hysteria. Joanne looked at where the ski-lift station had been. It was the one Marie-Claire and Bernard would have used. They could have been coming down by it. . .

Daniel's mouth was grim. He was thinking similar thoughts to hers. Then he said in a calm, authoritative voice, 'We'd better see about helping where we can.' He looked steadily into her face and gripped her arms hard,

willing her not to panic, trying to give her courage. 'Good
girl!' he said, as a small smile flickered on her lips.

In no time Joanne was galvanised into action. She was a
nurse. Daniel was a doctor. Their skills were going to be
needed urgently, perhaps tested as never before. Heaven
knew how many people might be buried under the snow.
Joanne forced herself not to think of Marie-Claire and
Bernard. There was nothing she could do but hope.

Daniel said, 'I'll find out what's happening, you do what
you can here. We'll have to set up a hospital somewhere.
There isn't one here, but there are bound to be emergency
medical supplies somewhere.'

The next few hours were an eternity Joanne never
wanted to experience again. She had been trained to cope
with emergencies, she had attended lectures on disasters,
she knew all about shock and trauma, but nothing had
prepared her for the reality.

In some amazing way, people organised themselves.
Although disasters like this rarely happened, the Swiss
were always prepared, so Daniel told her during a brief
reunion when they had set up a first aid station in a
guesthouse near the hotel. Already victims were being dug
out of the snow and brought in for treatment.

Ambulances could not get through by road yet as the
road down the mountain had been cut off and the weather
was too bad for helicopters to come in and take out the
injured. They would have to manage as best they could
until morning. Fortunately the avalanche had only sliced
across one end of the village, damaging a number of
buildings including one of the ski-lift stations and burying
the car park.

There were medical supplies, but they were scarcely
adequate for the number of people requiring treatment.
As the night wore on a steady stream of victims came or
were brought on stretchers to the makeshift hospital.

Some had only minor injuries, some were seriously hurt. Joanne realised that she was the only nurse in the village. There was a local doctor who was luckily unhurt and between the three of them she, the doctor and Daniel coped as best they could. There were plenty of willing hands to provide food and warm drinks, blankets, quilts and hot water bottles for the injured.

Once when Joanne was checking the drip on a seriously hurt man with suspected internal injuries, she suddenly found Daniel at her side. 'How's he doing?' Daniel asked anxiously.

'Touch and go,' she answered.

'If you can keep him going till morning, he might pull through,' Daniel whispered. He raked his hand wearily through his tousled hair. 'Thank goodness there's no one else in quite such a bad way. Yet,' he added gravely, and they looked at each other without saying what was in both their minds. The search for victims would continue through the night and by morning more casualties would undoubtedly be found. The longer it took to find people, the worse condition they were likely to be in.

'Most of the injuries so far seem to be broken bones and concussion, cuts and bruising,' said Joanne. 'And a few cases of hypothermia.'

Daniel said, 'The lower part of the ski-lift was swept away. We probably won't know until daylight if anyone was trapped in the chairs.' Again their thoughts were expressed in the anguish of their eyes. Neither wanted to mention Marie-Claire and Bernard. Joanne was convinced they had been caught in the avalanche, either as they skied back into the village or returned in the ski-lift.

She looked away suddenly, emotion threatening to overwhelm her. Daniel's fingers encircled her arm. 'People can survive in snowdrifts, Joanne,' he said, and she knew he was trying to convince himself as much as her. She looked up at him, keeping her lips tightly pressed together to stop them trembling. He tucked a strand of hair behind her ear, touching her temple with a soothing stroke.

'It's going to be a long night, I'm afraid,' he said.

And it was. There would never be a night so long in all the rest of her life, Joanne felt sure. Sometimes she glanced at Daniel as she helped him bandage, suture, or fix splints on limbs, and marvelled at how perfectly they worked together as a team. She had slipped back into emergency ward routine automatically, and it was obvious Daniel had not forgotten his training as a general practitioner either.

As though reading her mind, he glanced up from binding a temporary splint and said, 'You must have done a stint on Casualty, I suppose, in your student days.'

'Many times. And as a staff nurse too. Even Saturday night was never like this, though!' She looked around at the makeshift beds and stretchers crammed into the room. 'It's like a battlefield!'

As the night wore on, Joanne found herself with more time to spare for talking to people and reassuring them. Most of the victims were skiers and tourists who had come to Blumenplatz for a late-season holiday. There was some delayed shock and sometimes outbursts of hysteria. Especially anxious were those who had been unable to locate friends or relatives.

Some people, like Joanne and Daniel, Marie-Claire and Bernard, had only come for the day. Joanne, whenever she had time, tried to find missing people and bring friends and relatives together, and that relieved a great deal of the tension. Those who were unhurt or only superficially injured were eager to help, but even so, the task was a big one and the strain enormous.

It was the early hours of the morning when Joanne, almost dead on her feet, suddenly stumbled slightly as she brought a fresh supply of bandages to Daniel. He caught her and steadied her, looking anxiously into her face.

'You'd better get some rest, Joanne. You're all in.'

'No, I'm fine, truly,' she insisted, fighting the weariness that had almost overcome her.

'Doctor's orders,' he said firmly. 'Lie down for a couple of hours. You're suffering from shock too, don't forget. You're no good to us half asleep!'

'What about you?' He was looking tired and haggard too.

'I'll take a short cat-nap soon. I think we've done just about all we can for now.'

Still the unspoken thought hung between them. Daniel clasped her hand and squeezed it, and Joanne squeezed back. No casualties had been brought in for some time now, but they mustn't give up hope yet, Joanne thought, they simply mustn't.

Taking Daniel's advice, she grabbed a couple of spare blankets and found a spot where she could curl up for an hour or two. She knew Daniel would rouse her if she was needed urgently. She woke to a loud noise and jumped up in a fright. Not another avalanche, surely? But as sleep fell away and she realised that it was growing light, she also recognised the staccato sound.

'A helicopter!' she exclaimed, and rushed to find Daniel.

The sky was still overcast, but it was no longer snowing and the chill wind had eased. The sudden blizzard that had taken everyone by surprise was over. Joanne gazed out at the chaos caused by the avalanche and her throat constricted. Were Marie-Claire and Bernard buried under all that snow?

'No!' she whispered. 'No. . .please. . .'

Medical help arrived with the helicopter, and the most seriously injured were carried on board to be ferried out to hospital. The road to the village was still impassable, Joanne learned, but tractors were already busy clearing away the snow, so access for road ambulances should be possible soon.

As the new team took over, Daniel said to Joanne, 'You can go back in the helicopter if you like, Joanne.'

She was sure he didn't really want her to and she certainly didn't want to go herself. 'No, Daniel, I'll stay with you. They need the room for the injured anyway.'

His hand clamped tightly on her shoulder, acknowledging gratitude for her support. Tight-lipped, he said, 'I'm not needed here now. I'm going out with the search parties.'

'I'll come to,' Joanne said at once.

'No! I'm not having you risk. . .'

'I'm coming,' she insisted, with fierce determination. 'We're going to look for Marie-Claire and Bernard together.'

He smiled at her with admiration. She was a plucky one all right, but he couldn't let her go. The others probably wouldn't allow it anyway.

'Joanne,' he said, 'you don't have the necessary experience and you can be of more use here. There are still people needing reassurance, and you're good at soothing the anxious.'

Joane reluctantly agreed. She knew too that he didn't want her to be there if they found Marie-Claire and Bernard and they were not alive. He wanted to spare her that.

As the first search party, with Daniel, set off, Joanne scanned the mountain. It looked so peaceful in the dawn light, with not even a scar to betray where the snow had broken away and plummeted down unimpeded even by the snow barriers. Fresh snow lay over the ski-runs and the jet black choughs wheeled and called in the crisp morning air.

In the other direction lay the graphic evidence of the

avalanche, the wrecked buildings, the distorted landscape where the road had been. Rescue teams were swarming over the mounds of snow searching for victims who might still be trapped beneath its innocent whiteness.

A second helicopter arrived, and as it hovered over the snow Joanne ran back to help with shifting out the patients who were to go next. She was watching the helicopter take off some minutes later when a man appeared and placed a hand on her shoulder.

'You are something of a heroine, I gather.'

She turned to find Klaus Reinhardt at her side, and found that she was not at all pleased.

'How did you get here?' she asked incredulously.

'I came in the helicopter.' He looked taken aback at her sharp tone. She was emotional, of course. 'I managed to cadge a lift.' He smiled. 'I couldn't miss a story like this!'

'Couldn't you?' Joanne said tartly, and started to walk away. When he followed her, she shook his hand off her arm and rounded on him. 'Is that all you're interested in, a good story?'

He couldn't understand her mood, naturally. He didn't know how deeply she was racked because of Marie-Claire and Bernard.

'I thought you might like to give me a few personal insights,' he explained. 'You must have had a tough night. Were there any fatalities? Some people are still missing, I believe.'

Joanne looked blankly at him. 'Yes, it was a tough night,' she said, 'and I don't want to talk about it.'

She turned sharply away from him, and when he tried to plead with her, she again shook off his hand and said, 'Leave me alone, please!'

Then she stopped dead and her hands flew to her face and her mouth opened in amazement, but no sound came out. Three people were coming towards her. One was

Daniel, with another man who was supporting a woman, and there was no doubt as to their identities.

'Marie-Claire! Bernard!' Joanne flung herself at them, feeling her heart would burst with relief and happiness. 'Oh—oh—oh!' There was nothing else she could say Her voice was choked with sobs as they clung together helplessly for several minutes.

'We thought you must. . .' Joanne said at last. 'But you're not. Oh, isn't it wonderful!'

She could scarcely believe it. They were apparently uninjured. Marie-Claire was weeping and laughing together.

'We were so afraid you might have been. . .' She hugged Joanne. 'It was terrible—not knowing.'

A few minutes later, over hot drinks and food, Bernard and Marie-Claire explained what had happened.

'Marie-Claire was fantastic,' said Bernard, holding tightly to her hand. 'She was so brave.' Marie-Claire laid her head against his shoulder as he went on, 'We were a long way from the ski-lift when the weather suddenly started closing in. There were several of us, and that blizzard struck so suddenly we were caught. We managed to reach the ski-lift, but before we could use it, the avalanche struck.

'We couldn't see the village because of the snow, but we knew the avalanche had put the ski-lift out of action. What other damage had been done we could only guess at. It would have been too dangerous to attempt to come down in the blizzard, so we took shelter in the hut up there. We were all frantic with worry about what had happened down here. It was a night I never want to live through again. We were all very tense, and a couple of them went to pieces. There was a couple who had young children down here. It was terrible for them. But Marie-Claire was superb. She was frantic with worry too, but she reassured everyone else, made hot drinks, heated up soup—there were emergency supplies in the hut, of course— and even had us singing songs. She really kept our spirits up.'

'She's worn out now, poor girl,' said Daniel, his eyes soft, and Joanne saw that Marie-Claire was now fast asleep on Bernard's shoulder.

Bernard said in a low voice, 'I was afraid the trauma— that it might bring back the horror of Paolos's accident, especially as it's so near the anniversary, and especially if you two were. . .' He shook his head wonderingly. 'But I think she's just tired now, exhausted mentally and physically.' He grinned sheepishly. 'I guess I am too—I'm not talking straight. You two must be dead on your feet.'

Daniel said thoughtfully in low tones so as not to wake his sister, 'Maybe she coped because she didn't feel so helpless. She was able to do something. When Paolo died she could do nothing. And this time she felt no guilt, no personal involvement in the same sense.'

Bernard nodded. 'She was trying to keep her mind off what might have happened to you, but as nearly everyone with us had somebody close down here, she learned a new perspective too.'

Daniel said, 'You'd better take her home as soon as you can, Bernard.' He left them to assist the other doctors, and Joanne said to Bernard,

'You love her very much, don't you, Bernard?'

His face said it all.

'Is there any chance. . .?' Joanne ventured. This shared experience might well have brought them closer together.

'I hope,' he said softly. 'My God, Joanne, I hope!'

Joanne pressed his hand. 'She needs you, Bernard.'

'We all need someone,' he said simply, and Joanne felt as though her heart would break. She needed Daniel, but Daniel would never need her. He had called her *Liebling* in a moment of calamity, and she would never forget it, but she knew it didn't mean anything, not the way she wanted it to.

In a few days the avalanche was almost history. It had made the headlines briefly, but as no one had actually been killed, not with any great dramatic impact.

'Why is it that disaster is more newsworthy than miracles?' complained Joanne disgustedly. 'Just because no one was killed or died from injuries, the papers dismiss it as though it was nothing. And some people were, after all, quite seriously hurt.'

She was back at work at the clinic and talking to Esther, who shrugged and said, 'We're a ghoulish lot, I suppose.'

On the second Wednesday after the avalanche, when Daniel was in Berne, and Joanne was in his study typing minor alterations to a few pages which he had asked her to do, the phone rang. Joanne answered it.

'Joanne?' Her heart leapt as she heard Daniel's voice.

'Yes.'

'I hoped you'd be there. Slaving away at my notes, are you?'

'I am. Is there something you want altered?'

'Er—I'm not sure—I was thinking about something I might have explained badly. Would you read me the begining of Chapter Two?'

He sounded very odd, Joanne thought, but she did as he asked. There was a moment's silence after he had told her to stop, and then he said, 'No, it sounds all right. Sorry to have worried you.'

'There's nothing you'll want re-drafted, then?'

'No...'

She thought he would ring off then, but he said questioningly, 'Joanne...?'

'I'm still here.'

There was another odd kind of silence as though he was

deliberating about something. Joanne prompted, 'Is there something else?'

'No—no, it doesn't matter. It'll keep.'

'You're sure? I've got plenty of time if there's anything else you want typed. You can dictate it over the phone if you like.'

'No, nothing like that. I was just going to. . .discuss something with you. I'll do it when I get home. You'll be in on Friday evening?'

'Of course I will. Early on. I'm on night duty, though.'

He rang off, leaving Joanne feeling slightly puzzled. He had sounded almost nervous. What about? she wondered. It was very strange.

The following afternoon she used the typewriter to write a couple of personal letters. She had spoken to Terri and her father on the phone after the ordeal at Blumenplatz, but Terri would be looking for a letter giving all the details, she knew.

She was just typing the envelope when she heard a car outside. Joanne thought nothing of it, assuming Elke or Fräulein Müller would answer the bell to whoever it was calling. However, the bell did not ring, and the next thing Joanne knew was the door being flung open and Daniel striding in. She turned around in amazement.

'Daniel!' His unexpected appearance brought a flush of colour to her cheeks.

He flung his briefcase into a chair. He looked grim, and Joanne was instantly anxious.

'What's wrong?' she asked. 'You're not ill, are you?' Then she realised that he was furious about something.

He opened his briefcase and took out a magazine. He slammed it down in front of her. 'That's what wrong!'

She stared unseeingly for a moment, and then the realisation of what she was looking at hit her. The picture on the front cover was a photograph of Marie-Claire and her embracing. They were wearing ski clothes. It had clearly been taken when Marie-Claire and Bernard returned after their night on the mountain. Across the bottom of it was a banner—EXCLUSIVE—and the screamer, 'Paolo Valli's widow in avalance drama—horror revisited.'

'Page three,' rasped Daniel. 'Go on, read all about it! You did a thorough job of filling him in, didn't you?' Only then did Joanne realise that his fury was directed at her.

Numb with shock, she turned the pages and saw the lead story, complete with pictures of Marie-Claire, Paolo Valli, the racing-car crash which had killed Paolo, a weeping Marie-Claire, the house, the clinic—it was all there. Horrified, she read the journalist's name in bold type— Klaus Reinhardt.

She glanced up at Daniel, white-faced. 'But...' She tried to speak, but he wouldn't let her.

He cut across her grittily, 'One of my partners saw it first. I went out and bought a copy. Not only has he dragged up all the details of Paolo's death, he's dramatised Marie-Claire's collapse and made some pretty blatant innuendoes as to her present condition. He's also brought in the clinic, mentioning names of patients being treated there and what for, and he's hinted at future articles full of titillating information. He could only have got his information from an inside source. How much did he pay you, Joanne?'

The question hit her like a blast from a furnace. 'Pay?' she echoed, bewildered. 'Are you joking, Daniel? I didn't tell Klaus any of this.'

'Didn't you?' he said scathingly. 'It seems pretty clear from the article that he talked to someone. And you don't deny you know him—I've seen him with you. He was even at Blumenplatz talking to you, getting an exclusive on the avalanche. He's handy with a camera too, apparently! Oh, it's quite pretty what he says about you, Joanne, even though he doesn't mention your name. But when I got hold of him and asked him, he admitted eventually that you were the source of his information.'

Joanne gasped at the lie, but worse was that Daniel was accusing her of breaking a trust. He surely didn't believe that she would do such a thing? Yet here was the evidence. Her eyes ran down a few paragraphs and she felt her heart sink. She would never be able to convince him that she had not provided Klaus with all this information.

Nevertheless, she said firmly, 'I didn't tell him anything. I refused to talk to him even at Blumenplatz.'

'Did you?' he sneered. 'I saw you myself! I think you told him everything he wanted to know, but you won't tell him any more. I've threatened a law-suit if he prints a word more about the clinic or Marie-Claire. I suppose you thought you were safe, that none of us would be likely to see such a dreadful rag as this is.'

Joanne looked at him in bleak despair. The pain and disappointment in his eyes made it even worse. He believed she had let him down unforgivably.

He drew an envelope out of his briefcase and handed it to her. 'Your air ticket to London and a cheque to cover your salary due and wages in lieu of notice. Go and pack. I'll drive you to Berne. I want you out of the way before you can do any more damage. Fortunately Marie-Claire doesn't usually see rubbish like this magazine, but perhaps you should just stop and remember for a moment what the consequences might be if she were to. It could undo all the good that's been done, especially now at this time, when Paolo's death is certainly in her mind.' The pain in his eyes was excruciating as he said, 'Joanne, how could you have done it. . .'

'Daniel, I. . .' she began, but he refused to listen.

'Go and pack. There isn't much time.'

Joanne had no choice. She ran upstairs, blinded by tears. How could it have ended like this? How could he not believe her? She could hear Marie-Claire's television, which she was thankful for. She crept into her own room and flung her clothes and other belongings willy-nilly into her suitcase, holdall and a couple of capacious carrier bags, cramming it all in wildly as the tears streamed down her face. Then, after she had removed the air ticket and put it in her handbag, she placed the envelope Daniel had given her, still containing his cheque, on the dressing table. She would tell him at the last minute that she did not want the money.

As she glanced around the room to make sure she had forgotten nothing, the door opened and Daniel stood there glowering impatiently.

'I'm coming,' Joanne said tightly.

He grabbed the suitcase from her hand. 'I'll take that!' he rapped out, and as his fingers brushed hers, the shock of his touch ran through her like wildfire. Nothing could change the way he affected her, not even his anger. She followed him, dry-eyed now, down to the car, and as they drove away she did not even glance back.

CHAPTER TEN

ALMOST before she knew what was happening, Joanne was on the plane. Despite his anger, Daniel had been polite to the last, escorting her to the departure area, seeing that she checked in and her luggage was taken care of. Then he had bidden her a brusque goodbye and turned and left her. Joanne remembered then that she had forgotten to tell him about the cheque she had left behind. But that didn't even matter now.

She watched his retreating figure with such an ache in her heart she thought she would die. It was over. He had never even remotely been hers to love, but she had loved him, would always love him, despite the cruel way he had misjudged her. She could forgive him for that. The evidence was very strong and his need to protect Marie-Claire overrode everything else.

At Zurich she had time to kill while waiting for her connection to London, and browsing on a bookstall, she saw the magazine Daniel had shown her. Although it was distasteful to her, she bought a copy, since she had not had time to read exactly what Klaus had written.

She sat down with a cup of coffee and read through the offending article. He could have garnered the details of the avalanche from a number of different people who probably didn't even know who Marie-Claire was, but because it made a better story he had attributed it all to one person. But how had he obtained details of Marie-Claire's breakdown, and also information about clients at the clinic? He must have waylaid someone else when Joanne had been uncooperative. Whoever it was had evidently let him think that Marie-Claire was being treated there, or else he had jumped to that conclusion.

'Please don't let Marie-Claire see it,' Joanne whispered to herself. Publicity like this could, as Daniel feared, wreck all the progress she had made. And especially at this delicate time when all the horror of Paolo's death must surely be vividly in her mind again. But fortunately it was not one of the magazines Marie-Claire regularly read, so there was a good chance she would never know about it.

Back in London, Joanne did not go straight home. She had not been able to warn them of her coming, and besides, she felt too churned up to make explanations. During the flight she toyed with alternative stories to explain her leaving, but nothing sounded convincing, so she decided to tell the truth.

She stayed the night in a London hotel—not the same one at which she and Daniel had stayed such a short time ago, but nevertheless it brought back poignant memories, and she spent a restless and miserable night.

The next day Joanne telephoned Terri, who was astonished, but delighted at first to hear that she was in London again so soon. Something in Joanne's voice, however, made her add, 'Is anything wrong? You're not ill, are you?'

'No, there's nothing wrong with me,' Joanne said hastily. 'I'm perfectly all right. I'll explain when I see you. Is it all right if I come down right away?'

'Joanne! Of course it's all right. I'll meet your train,' said Terri.

On the way home from the station, Joanne told Terri as briefly as possible what had happened. It was hard to keep her emotion in check as she talked, and it all still seemed like a bad dream from which she would awaken any moment. After she had finished, Terri was silent for a few moments and Joanne's heart thudded nervously. Didn't she believe her?

At last Terri said, 'Sorry—I'm just so stunned. Joanne, it's awful! Oh, what can you do? It does look like a no-win situation.' She turned a grim glance to her stepdaughter. 'You could sue that journalist, perhaps.'

Joanne shook her head. 'He's already told Daniel I gave him information. He didn't like me for refusing to have anything to do with him, especially that morning at Blumenplatz. I was a bit uptight, naturally, and I was very short with him.'

'I don't blame you. But have you any idea who did give him information?'

Again Joanne shook her head. 'It could have been anybody. I'm sure it wasn't Bernard, but I couldn't be sure about anyone else. Esther, Gerda, Anton, any one of the nurses could be guilty, so could some of the domestic staff. Quite a lot of people know about Marie-Claire and most would respect her privacy, I'm sure, but if Klaus was snooping around and offering money for information, anyone might have been tempted.' She sighed. 'And even if I have a strong suspicion, I doubt that Daniel or Luise would believe me. It would be my word against theirs, and Klaus's.'

'You're probably right,' Terri said gravely. 'But I wish there was something we could do.'

'Don't worry about it,' said Joanne, attempting to sound nonchalant. 'It really doesn't matter. So long as Marie-Claire never sees that magazine, there'll be no harm done.'

Terri slid her a sly glance as they pulled up at a set of traffic lights. 'I thought you were rather fond of Daniel.'

Joanne tried in vain to stem the deep colour flooding into her cheeks. 'No, Terri, you're wrong about that,' she lied, and knew it sounded unconvincing. As they arrived at the house, Joanne asked, 'How's the baby?'

Terri grinned contentedly. 'He's as good as gold! Or she is!'

As they entered her old home, Joanne thought how lucky she was still to have this refuge.

That evening, when the story had been told again to her father, he was as indignant as Terri.

'I'm surprised at Daniel! He seemed such a nice man. I wouldn't have thought he'd condemn and pass sentence without hearing both sides of the case.'

'There weren't two sides, so far as he could see,' said Joanne dismally. 'Let's face it, what could I say to defend myself? I could only deny it.'

'It's grossly unfair,' Terri put in. 'After all Joanne did for Marie-Claire. That should have been enough to tell him she couldn't possibly betray her like that.'

Joanne shook her head sadly. 'He was very upset about it. I think he was finding it hard to believe that I would do such a thing. But he's frightened for Marie-Claire, Terri. You can't blame him. He's already had one tragedy in his life. And he dotes on Marie-Claire. Because she's so much younger, he's very protective of her. Her welfare is more important than anything else.'

Her father said gently, 'You'll stay here with us, of course, Joanne.'

She nodded. 'Thanks, I'd like to, for a while anyway. I must decide what I want to do next. I mustn't sit around feeling sorry for myself.' She lifted her chin bravely. 'Maybe I'll take a job in darkest Africa!'

Terri frowned at the flippancy. 'Why don't you go back to the Lord Barmouth? I'm sure they'd snap you up, and then you'd be able to live at home like you did before.'

In the end Joanne did go back to nursing at the Barmouth, but she did not live at home. She had made up her mind not to do that before, and so she moved into the nurses' home despite strong opposition from her father and Terri.

'No,' she insisted, 'I'd rather live at the hospital. This is your home now, and you need your privacy. I'd love to come for weekends sometimes, and I hope you'll let me baby-sit sometimes!'

Joanne was putting a brave face on her troubles, but Terri was sure she was not nearly as cheerful as she pretended. Terri suspected that Joanne's misery was as much because of Daniel himself as the false accusations made against her. She sighed and said to her husband every now and then, 'Poor Joanne! I think her heart's broken since that Swiss business. I do wish you could find someone. . .'

Joanne slipped easily back into nursing at the Lord Barmouth and sometimes she wondered if she had ever been away, if the Swiss interlude had been no more than a dream. But alone at night in her small flat in the nurses' home, it was all too real. She could will herself not to think of Switzerland or Daniel during the day when she was busy, but at night the more she tried to forget, the more she remembered.

She was just going off duty one afternoon, and was passing through the entrance foyer of the hospital to post some letters in the box there, when she heard a male voice call her name.

For a split second she thought it was Daniel and her heart constricted, but as she turned round she saw how wrong she was. 'Luke!' she exclaimed.

'Joanne!' He clasped her shoulders and looked into her face. 'How good to see you again. As lovely as ever, I see.'

Her heart should have been fluttering, but it wasn't. She just felt choked with rage and disappointment. How dared he say such things after months and months of no word at all? 'You're back,' she muttered.

'A couple of weeks ago,' he told her gaily. 'I came down

today to see about a job—and to see you too, of course.'

'Of course,' she said dryly.

Two weeks, she thought, he's been back two weeks and he hasn't bothered to contact me. Even if he had been with his family in the Midlands, he could still have phoned. . . But he probably wouldn't have bothered to see her today, she thought, if it hadn't happened accidentally. He had never really cared about her, that was plain. And I can't imagine how I ever thought I cared about him, she thought.

'You'll have to excuse me, Luke,' she said hastily. 'I've got rather a lot to do.'

Such a weak excuse was hardly likely to rebuff him, and it didn't. He held her a little away from him. 'Not too much to stop you having dinner with me tonight, I hope?' He was turning on the charm now, certain she wouldn't say no. 'We've got so much to talk about. I'll pick you up at seven-thirty. You're still at Highfield Grove?'

'No, I'm living at the nurses' home now,' she said in a flat tone.

'Ah, so you've cut the apron strings at last.'

His tone nettled her and she answered sharply, 'As I wrote and told you, my father married again.'

'Yes, so you did,' he murmured, and drew her towards him and kissed her rather hard on the mouth, a kiss that aroused not the slightest response in any part of her. 'I'll pick you up there, then,' he said confidently.

'Luke, I really don't think. . .' she began, but he was insistent.

'Joanne—we've got a lot of time to make up!'

'Have we?' she said, her mouth twisting ironically. He didn't even notice. She did not want to make a scene in a public place, so she weakened. 'All right—seven-thirty. Flat Three.

She would make it very clear to Luke tonight that he no longer had any place in her life. She had no intention of drifting into a casual relationship with Luke again. He only wanted one with no strings attached. No, she meant to keep clear of Luke—of all men, in fact. There was less misery in being lonely than in having your heart broken.

Joanne wished later she hadn't said she would have dinner with Luke. She dressed in the grey wool dress that she had bought in Berne, as it was a cool evening, and she was almost ready when the doorbell rang. She smiled to herself. Luke must be keen—he was early for once! She went reluctantly to open it, longing for the evening to be over, and her greeting to Luke was half said before she realised it wasn't him.

'Daniel!' She felt such a surge of emotion that she almost crumpled at his feet as she had done so embarrassingly once before.

'May I come in?' He was smiling a little anxiously. 'I want to talk to you.'

'I—I'm just going out,' Joanne said faintly.

His grey-blue eyes looked her over slowly. 'Yes, I can see you must be, but what I have to say won't take long.'

'All right.'

She did not invite him to sit down. What could he possibly want to say to her? She faced him stoically, determined not to let him see the warmth she felt for him.

'Well, what do you want?' she asked, keeping her tone icy. Her heart was beating rapidly. Could it be something to do with Marie-Claire that had brought him here, something else for which he held her responsible? She waited apprehensively for his answer.

'You have a date, I presume?'

'Yes, I'm going out to dinner.' Joanne glanced at her watch. 'He'll be here any minute. Perhaps it could wait...' She didn't want to wait, however, she wanted to know now why he had come.

Daniel obviously felt uneasy standing up, but still she

didn't invite him to sit down. She felt less vulnerable somehow with them both standing. He shifted slightly, glanced around the room, and then his eyes came back to her face.

'I have to apologise, Joanne,' he said, and she caught her breath, 'I acted hastily. I have a tendency, as you know, to overreact sometimes. . .' A faint smile hovered on his lips and she remembered with a pang the time she had unintentionally insulted him. So long ago now, yet still so vivid in her mind!

He went on, 'I wrongly accused you of revealing confidential information to Klaus Reinhardt. I know now it wasn't you, and also that you didn't even talk to him at Blumenplatz after the avalanche.'

Joanne wished she had asked him to sit down. She felt weak at the knees. It was unbelievable, but it must be true. Somehow he had found out the truth. A wave of thankfulness swept over her and brought tears to her eyes. 'How do you know?' she asked in a whisper.

Daniel laid his fingertips tentatively on her shoulders and looked deeply into her eyes. 'I don't know how to say adequately how sorry I am.'

'Daniel, don't—it doesn't matter. I'm just relieved you found out the truth. But how? And who did talk to Klaus?'

'Gerda Volker.'

'Gerda! No—really? I knew it had to be someone from the clinic, but I couldn't decide who. Why did she do it?'

'Money, of course. Klaus paid her very well for her information.'

Joanne nodded. 'Of course—she was always short of money, always complaining about it. Esther used to get angry with her because she didn't seem to have the least idea how to manage her salary.'

'It was Esther who made me have second thoughts,' he admitted. 'Her and Marie-Claire. When Esther remarked that Gerda must have either inherited, or be earning money in her spare time because she'd just bought a car, an unpleasant little niggle began in the back of my mind.

'I wasn't happy with Gerda's performance, and neither was my mother, but we were loath to dismiss her. She's young and has a lot to learn, but I don't think nursing suits her temperament. When I became suspicious, I talked to her, remarked on the car and asked how she afforded it. She talked vaguely about a boyfriend, not dreaming of course that I would connect his name with the journalist who had caused the clinic a good deal of trouble.

'I was almost sure then that I'd done you a grave injustice. I tackled Klaus Reinhardt again and after a certain amount of pressure, he admitted the truth. He'd got nowhere with you, so he'd tried someone else. Gerda was very co-operative when he mentioned money, and told her also that if there was trouble, he would make sure you got the blame. She also thought it was unlikely that any of us would ever see the articles. She's not intelligent enough to see the kind of repercussions such revelations might have, I'm afraid.'

Joanne sank on to the arm of the nearest lounge chair. 'I see. Gerda never liked me. I think she was jealous because I lived at your house and Bernard took me skiing.'

Daniel nodded. 'Yes, that's probably so.' He seemed to be having as much difficulty controlling his emotions as she was now. It couldn't be easy for him to admit he had been wrong, she thought, and she felt sorry for him.

'Thank you for coming personally to tell me,' she said, and asked urgently, 'How is Marie-Claire?'

'Much improved. She sends her love.'

'I'm so glad she's still improving,' Joanne said thankfully. 'And I'm glad she never did see that dreadful article.'

Daniel astonished her, saying, 'But she did! She picked up the magazine in a hairdressing salon in Berne. Yes—she went to have her hair done for the first time in a year! She told me about it afterwards. She said it was a shock at first, but then it was like reading about another person. It didn't affect her in any adverse way at all. I think she realised then that she was almost completely recovered. She can look at any part of her life now and not want to close it off, or blame anyone else for it. She isn't afraid any more. It was after she saw the story that she began to suspect the real reason you'd left. When she told me about it, I had to admit I'd already seen the article.'

'What had you told her before?' asked Joanne. How Marie-Claire must have felt about her sudden departure had always worried her. She knew Daniel could not have told her the truth, and because she didn't know what he had told his sister, she could not write to her.

'I told her you had family problems and had to go home in a hurry. She was very puzzled, naturally, and a bit hurt because you'd said nothing to her and you didn't write.'

'I couldn't. . .' Joanne explained. 'I didn't know what you'd told her, and I knew you would prefer me not to have any more to do with her.'

'Don't worry, she understands now. She was extremely angry with me when I explained!' Daniel smiled a little ruefully. 'She refused to believe me, and we didn't speak to each other for some days! It was because of my own doubts and Marie-Claire's that I finally talked to Gerda and then winkled the truth out of Klaus. I'm sorry it took so long.'

Joanne drew in a deep breath and let it out slowly. She said again, 'It was good of you to come, Daniel. I'm thankful to have my name cleared.'

'There's something else I want to say,' he went on hesitantly.

Was he going to ask her to return to the clinic? Joanne wondered. She wouldn't go, of course. Every cell in her body longed to be back where she could at least see him every day, or nearly every day, even if she didn't live at his mother's house, but she knew that would be inflicting a futile torture.

He said, with a deeply penetrating look, 'Marie-Claire said there was a very good reason why, despite all the evidence, you couldn't possibly be guilty. I want to know if she was right.'

Joanne was nonplussed. 'What was the reason?'

'Joanne...' He moved towards her, and as he did so the doorbell rang again. Daniel looked startled as though he had forgotten she was going out. 'Your date, I suppose?' he muttered.

Joanne went to the door.

'Hello, darling! Wow, you look fabulous!' Before she could stop him Luke was whirling her round in his arms and kissing her with fervour. The sweep-her-off-her-feet approach, she thought wryly.

Before she could say anything he was saying, 'Joanne, you don't know how I've missed you! Isn't it wonderful to be together again! Tell me you've missed me too.'

Joanne struggled in his arms, certain now that Luke had noticed Daniel and was performing for his benefit. Now he pretended surprise. 'Oh—sorry, I didn't realise...' He eyed Daniel suspiciously.

Joanne's face was flaming with embarrassment and anger. She mumbled an introduction. Daniel, his face a grim mask, said, 'Is this your doctor friend who went overseas?'

She could only say, 'Yes,' remembering how she had let Daniel believe there was more to the relationship than there actually was.

'I just got back from Canada,' said Luke, 'and with a bit of luck I'll be working at the Lord Barmouth again soon.' He clasped Joanne's hand possessively. 'It's great to be picking up the threads again.' He looked Daniel over speculatively, obviously wondering what place he might have in Joanne's life, and presumably with some idea of disposing of any claim on her, added, 'Absence always make the heart grow fonder, doesn't it? That's what Joanne said when I went away, and it's certainly proved to be true—for both of us.' He smiled down into her face and she could have hit him. But what did it matter if Daniel went on believing what she'd told him?

Daniel said through tight lips, 'Yes, it certainly does.'

Joanne pulled away from Luke. 'Daniel, you were in the middle of telling me about Marie Claire. . .' she said, curious to know why Marie-Claire had been so sure she wasn't guilty.

Daniel gave her an odd look. 'I think she must have been wrong,' he said, adding abruptly, 'Do write to her. She'd like to know you're well and happy.'

He left quickly, and Luke asked, 'Who was that? He looked a bit ruffled. You haven't been two-timing me, I hope, darling!'

Joanne's patience ran out. 'And I suppose you've been celibate all this time! You didn't expect me to wait around like a grass widow for you, surely!' Anger made her raise her voice. 'You've got a nerve, Luke, waltzing back and thinking you can pick me up where you left off! You haven't even written to me for months and months. Well, let's get this straight now. You can't. What there was once between us doesn't exist any more. It's been finished for a long time. I'm sorry, I shouldn't have agreed to have dinner with you tonight. It was inevitable we would quarrel. I was going to tell you it was all over tonight, but I might as well do it now instead of spoiling your evening.'

'You just have!' he complained.

'I'm sorry. I'd hoped to be a bit more tactful about it.'

'Oh come on, Joanne,' he coaxed, 'let's go and have a drink first, and you can get it all off your chest in a civilised manner. I guess I do have some apologising to do.'

It was too late for apologies, and Joanne told him so. 'Please go now, Luke, I just want to be alone.'

He shrugged, hesitated for another moment, then turned on his heel and left her. Joanne sank down on to the couch and wept. Presently she got up and made a cup of tea, but having drunk it she felt worse than ever. The flat was suddenly claustrophobic. She needed company, someone to talk to, even if she couldn't talk about Daniel. After half an hour of indecision, she finally rang home.

'Terri, could I come round tonight?'

'Of course.' Terri sounded a bit puzzled for some reason. Her voice had an odd little catch in it as she said, 'We haven't eaten yet. If you hurry you can sit down with us.'

Joanne was uneasy. 'You haven't got visitors, have you? I don't want to intrude.'

Terri made a rather incomprehensible sound and said, 'Just come round, Joanne, right away. There's no problem.'

Joanne still felt doubtful. But she could hardly change her mind now. She asked the question that was burning in her mind. 'Terri, did Daniel Peterson contact you today to find out where I was?'

Terri did not answer for a moment, then said anxiously, 'You didn't mind my telling him, I hope. He said it was rather urgent.'

'No, I didn't mind. I'll tell you all about it when I see you.'

'Right-oh. Don't be long.'

Joanne, feeling a shade better already, flung on a jacket and dashed out to her car. She was parking in the driveway of her old home in Highfield Grove within minutes. Terri opened the door to her and greeted her warmly, but her manner was a little odd, Joanne thought. Something was definitely amiss.

'I'm sorry to barge in like this,' Joanne apologised. 'It is all right, isn't it?'

'Of course it's all right,' Terri insisted. 'How many times do I have to tell you? You've just time for a drink before dinner, so go and join Andrew in the living room while I take a peep in the oven,' The look she gave Joanne was definitely peculiar and she ran out to the kitchen as though she was escaping.

Joanne pushed open the living room door and went in. Her father was standing by the mantelpiece, a drink in his hand. He looked up as she came in.

'Ah, Joanne dear, I thought it must be you. You were quick. Come along in.'

It was only when the figure rose from the big winged armchair which, having its back to her, had hidden him from her view, that Joanne realised they had a visitor and who that visitor was.

'Daniel!' she exclaimed for the second time that evening, and her throat constricted in the same painful way as it had earlier.

'Hello again, Joanne.'

'What are you doing here?' She was perplexed.

'Lovely to see you,' said her father, pecking her cheek. 'Now you're here I can go and make a couple of urgent phone calls before dinner while you look after Daniel.'

He was gone before she could even open her mouth again, and Daniel was standing there smiling at her in a slightly bemused way. Neither said a word for a full minute, then Daniel murmured, 'Your father is a very tactful man!'

'But what are you doing here?' Joanne repeated. His nearness was sending her emotions into turmoil.

'I might ask the same question of you,' he countered. 'When I last saw you, you were on your way out with a rather possessive and abrasive young man called Luke.'

She flushed. 'I—I. . .' Suddenly tears filled her eyes and she couldn't go on. When Daniel's arms folded around her, strong and comforting, she was only able to murmur, 'Oh, Daniel. . .' in a tone of deep despair.

'Joanne, my love!' he whispered against her hair, but the words were surely only a cruel makebelieve. He said softly, 'Does this mean you're not in love with Luke after all?'

Numbly, she nodded. 'I was never in love with him—I only thought I was once. I was going to tell him tonight, but I ended up doing it rather sooner and more bluntly than I'd planned.'

'So you only pretended to be in love with someone when you told me. . .'

'Yes. . .' she confessed softly.

'Why, Joanne? Not just to get me out of your bedroom, surely?'

She buried her face against him. She would not tell him why just to boost his ego and have him feel sorry for her. He held her away from him a little and tilted her chin so that she had to meet his eyes. He began to smile faintly, then touched his lips to hers with a kiss so magic it kindled living fires all through her.

'Joanne, if he hadn't butted in I would have told you that I love you. . .'

'No. . .'

'What do you mean, no? It's the truth. I started falling in love with you from the moment I picked you up half frozen and somewhat bedraggled on the road to Interlaken, with snow sparkling on those long curling lashes and your pretty mouth all forlorn!' Daniel smoothed her hair tenderly. 'It was very difficult to resist you, and it seemed so unlikely you would ever love me—your feelings always seemed so superficial where I was concerned. And when I had to banish you from my life I was desolate. It was agony, even believing what I did about you. You can't imagine my joy when I found out I was wrong!'

'I can't believe. . .' Joanne whispered weakly.

'You must! Now, please tell me that what Marie-Claire said was true after all.'

'What did she say?'

'She said you couldn't possibly be guilty because you were in love with me, and nobody hurts the one they love, not like that. If only I'd had the courage to ask you to marry me that day I telephoned on a silly pretext—the day before . . .'

'Marry you!' exclaimed Joanne. There were firecrackers going off in her brain.

'Yes, *meine Liebling*. . . in spite of what you'd said in London about some doctor who was overseas, I was going to chance my arm. But I didn't have the nerve. I was so afraid you'd turn me down, so I decided to wait until I was face to face with you again, when I would use all my powers to persuade you.' Daniel held her close and went on in a taut voice, 'The next day I saw that magazine and I saw red! Can you imagine how I felt? There I was poised to ask you to marry me, head over heels in love with you, and I was confronted with that! Of course I overreacted! If only I'd known first that you truly loved me, perhaps I wouldn't have been so implacable.'

Joanne was looking at him with shining eyes. 'But, Daniel, if you were in love with me. . .all that time. . .what about Elise? I thought. . .'

'I told you about Elise!'

'But I thought, that night in London, that she'd rejected you, and that. . .well, you just wanted comfort. . .'

'Joanne! How could you think that of me?'

'I don't know. I'm sorry.'

He looked intently into her face. 'Is that the only reason you threw me out?'

She nodded. 'I couldn't bear to be a substitute.'

Daniel was aghast. 'You, *kleine Liebling*, a substitute? Never! Let me tell you about Elise. She and I are old friends, that's all. She helped me when I lost Ingrid. That was a very bad time for me, and she helped me to regain my perspective on life and forget. But she's been in love with Josef for some time. If it seemed I saw a lot of her, it was only because I was trying to help her as she'd helped me. She guessed, my love, that I was in love with you. She was the one who said I might get a pleasant surprise if I asked you to marry me!'

Joanne smiled. 'I feel a fool. I always seem to behave idiotically with you.'

He pressed her closer. 'Never!'

She chuckled suddenly. 'No wonder Terri seemed in a tizz when I rang! You told her I was going out with Luke, I suppose. And she probably was afraid I might not come if I knew you were here.'

'I was so despairing when I left you, I phoned Terri again and asked if she knew how serious you were about Luke. She knew nothing about him at all. She asked me to dinner, and your father remembered that Luke was an old flame, but he knew no more than that either.'

'Today was the first time I'd seen Luke since he went away. He stopped writing months ago, and he'd been back a fortnight and hadn't bothered to contact me. He never loved me any more than I loved him.'

'So you do love me, Joanne?' Daniel asked softly.

She drew his lips down close to hers. '*Ich liebe dich*, Daniel!'

'*Ach*, your German is perfect now!' he said. '*Ich liebe dich sehr*, Joanne.'

'And I love you very much too,' she replied, softly matching her lips to his.

'And you will marry me?'

'Try and stop me!'

He lifted her face in his strong palms. 'I would have been so lonely living in England if you'd said no!'

'In England? What do you mean?'

Daniel dragged his fingers through her hair and her whole body trembled. 'That's another thing I didn't get around to telling you, did I? It was part of what I was going to tell you when I phoned from Berne that day. I've decided to take my mother's advice and devote my time to the Foundation and maybe a practice in England. She's going to marry Karl Hoffmann, you know, and will probably give up the clinic. She's not as young as she used to be!'

'Daniel—but are you sure?' Joanne was overwhelmed.

'Quite sure. And if Marie-Claire and Bernard—well, we won't count our chickens yet, but the signs are promising.' He went on, 'Tell me you approve. I know you'd rather live in England and be near your family, and I know you prefer the Barmouth to the Harder-Kulm. . .' His eyes were lovingly teasing.

'That's not true! I loved it at the Harder-Kulm!'

'But your heart is in England, as part of mine is too. We can often go to Switzerland. It isn't far away, after all.'

Joanne looked at him with ever deepening love. 'You're doing this just for me, aren't you?'

Daniel held her tight. 'For both of us, *Liebling*. If you're happy, then I'll be happy too. Wherever we are.'

She wrapped her arms tightly around him and moulded her body as close to his as she could, as though to mingle their love in an indissoluble essence.

She raised her face to his and for a long moment they looked searchingly at each other, but there were no doubts now, nothing but love for each other. Daniel touched his lips to hers once more and told her in ways better than words what she already knew.

Terri opened the door of the living room very quietly and gently closed it again. She said to her husband, who was hovering at her elbow, 'It's all right, I think you've got time for another brandy before dinner! And I suspect we're going to have a good reason for opening a bottle of champagne!'